ONCE UPON
Eliza

- a novel –

Erynn

Mangum

Cover design by Paper and Sage Designs

Scripture taken from the NEW AMERICAN STANDARD BIBLE®, Copyright © 1960, 1962, 1963, 1968, 1971, 1972, 1973, 1975, 1977, 1995 by The Lockman Foundation. Used by permission.

Scripture quotations from THE MESSAGE. Copyright © by Eugene H. Peterson 1993, 1994, 1995, 1996, 2000, 2001, 2002. Used by permission of NavPress. All rights reserved. Represented by Tyndale House Publishers, Inc.

OTHER NOVELS
BY ERYNN MANGUM

THE LAUREN HOLBROOK SERIES

Miss Match

Rematch

Match Point

Match Made

Bake Me A Match

THE MAYA DAVIS SERIES

Cool Beans

Latte Daze

Double Shot

THE PAIGE ALDER SERIES

Paige Torn

Paige Rewritten

Paige Turned

Erynn Mangum

To my little girl, Eisley Laine –
You cannot even begin to imagine the love I have for you.
No matter what happens in this life, you are loved, you are
delighted in and you are treasured. You are enough.
Never forget that, my precious girl!

CHAPTER *One*

Despite the Tanners and their happy little romp up the grassy hill during the *Full House* theme song, I could do without predictability. I've never been a fan of it. Most of my life hasn't contained very much of it, so it's probably for the best that I could do without it.

I look at the brand new mom who is about twenty-two in front of me and want to try to tell her to give up the good fight too. She's clinging onto the front of her hospital gown in a fairly futile effort to keep it together as I attempt to monitor her blood pressure and pulse. Based on the labeled bags she and her husband brought in and the checklist I saw laying on the foot of the bed next to her 14-hour old infant, I'm thinking this is a woman who likes some organization in her life.

I swear there's a line next to a little box on the checklist that reads, "*birth child*". And there's a checkmark in the box.

A small part of my soul might have just died.

There's organized and then there's you-need-medication.

I think we are officially flirting with that line.

"All right, Rachel, when was the last time you tried to breastfeed?" I ask.

She holds on to the front of her gown and reaches for the rolling table next to her bed and produces another sheet of paper. This one is a graph and she runs her finger down the page. "One fifty-seven this afternoon," she tells me.

Oh boy.

"Great!" I say, instilling some enthusiasm into my voice and not correcting her to two o'clock. "It's been about two hours then, so let's go ahead and try again. I'm going to have our lactation nurse come by later today too."

She nods. I pick up the baby and do a quick vitals check on the little boy as I hand him over to his mother. She reaches across to the table again and grabs a nursing cover.

"Actually, Rachel, I need to be able to see him latch," I say. Carrington Springs Grace Hospital is a great place to work but they put a lot of emphasis on first time mothers and breastfeeding success. I've only lived in Carrington Springs for a little less than a year and I can't even remember how many breastfeeding success seminars I've been to now.

Enough to make me never want to have children of my own. But watching these poor women come in here all battered and stitched and bleeding from childbirth is also a great form of birth control.

"Oh," Rachel says, and I try to be sympathetic to her need for some privacy after delivering a baby. I take the cover from her and carefully drape it around her shoulders so the only thing I'll be seeing is just the baby's latch and nothing else.

She holds the baby awkwardly, putting him in front of her breast and then just looking at him. She looks up at me.

"He doesn't seem to want to eat right now," she says.

"Well, I mean, he might not. But babies this young need a little more help," I tell her.

Ten minutes later, Baby Bryce is officially sucking, I can check the box on my chart and I write the time down for Rachel on her graph paper.

"I'll be back in a little bit. Do you need anything?"

She shakes her head. "When do I get to leave?"

"I don't have official release documents yet, but we like you guys to stay at least twenty-four hours just to monitor the bleeding."

She sighs. "Thanks Eliza."

"No problem."

I close the door behind me, make my notes on her chart and go to the next patient's room.

We have jokes about full moons and babies being born, but seriously, it's not just a wives' tale. We are almost completely booked up today. I have barely even seen my fellow nurses because we are running around so much after the influx of patients from last night. Even the hospital pediatricians, who normally are moving pretty slowly, are making time, hurrying through the neutral-colored walls as they race from the patients' rooms. I passed all the night shift delivery nurses in the elevators on my way in today and they looked like Will Smith at the end of one of his survival movies.

Seriously, though, should zombies or aliens or rabid ground hogs ever start attacking, I'm immediately finding Will Smith and heading straight for him. He's the only person who ever makes it out alive.

I've got a new patient that was just settled into the room next door to Rachel, so I go in to do my initial assessment of the mom and baby. This mama was a c-section delivery after eighteen hours of labor and she looks like it.

"Hi there, Becca, my name is Eliza and I'm going to be your nurse for the next few hours," I say, walking into the room and washing my hands and forearms in the sink.

Becca is holding the baby in a slightly reclined position on the bed and there's a man on his phone near the foot of the bed. He tells whomever he's talking to that the nurse is here and he'll call back. I smile at them both.

"What a beautiful baby," I say, peeking at the newborn little girl. "How are you feeling, Becca?"

"I'm in some pain," she tells me and based on the tenseness of her voice and the lines on her face, she doesn't have to convince me.

Sometimes I want to tell these mothers that the pain has only just begun, because after this they then get to deal with cracked and sore nipples, toddler tantrums and five year-olds who can be disrespectful in two languages, thanks to Dora the Explorer and her cousin Diego.

But I don't say anything.

Nursing is thirty percent medicine and seventy percent holding your tongue. Or your stomach, depending on the shift.

In nursing school, we did rounds on every floor and while most of my fellow students just yawned through the Mother Baby floor and made jokes about crocheting in the corner while passing out morphine, I totally came to life on this unit. I love the babies, I love the new mamas. I love getting to be a part of something so life altering in such a unique way. I see these patients at their absolute best and worst all at the same time. And never once in the almost year I've worked here have I ever had time to sit and crochet.

I spend the day running back and forth between my three patients and their babies. I bring drugs and saline, Colace and fresh pads. I remove two catheters and check three fundal heights multiple times. I snuggle one baby while the mama has a miniature breakdown and I hold another mom's hair back while she gets sick from the pain medicine. I change about twenty-three diapers and show one dad how to get the baby clean from the meconium.

It's busy.

But, seven o'clock comes and I haven't had one hemorrhage and no one has delivered a surprise twin, so it's a good day.

I have this recurring nightmare that I'll be going in to check the mom's fundal height and a baby will just plop right out on the sheets. For as much as I love them after they are born, I do not love babies when they are in the process of being born. Too much slime, too much yuck. And yes, I recognize that the odds of a surprise twin being born in the postpartum room are basically nil in today's world of ultrasounds and decent medicine, but still.

You never know. And Google just makes these things seem like they happen every day.

I click myself out on the computer and make sure my replacement, Ashley, doesn't have any last questions as I grab my purse from my locker.

"Have a good night, Eliza. Wait, you're off for a few days now, right?"

I nod. I just finished up three twelve-hour days. My brain needs the break. "Yep. So thankful."

"Got any big plans?"

"I'm painting my bedroom."

Ashley rolls her eyes. "Sounds restful."

Most of my fellow nurses on this floor are either moms themselves to small children or moms of older kids. Neither one of those groups seems to get my need to do something when I'm off, especially when I'm off for four days in a row.

I don't sit well.

Plus, painting is a perfect activity because I can just roll and not think about anything except getting the strokes even.

"It will be great. See you, Ashley!"

She waves and I head out. The days are getting longer, the bare trees I've been staring sadly at all winter are starting to bud and bloom. Spring is my absolute favorite season. I never understood why the New Year began in January when everything is dead. It should definitely begin in mid-March.

I climb into my car, drive home and it's completely dark outside when I get to my house. I finally learned after months of being creeped out coming home to a dark, empty house that I can buy a little timer for the front lamp and at least come home to a semi-lit house.

It makes it way less creepy.

I pull in the garage and look across the street at my friend Katie's house. Katie theoretically works from home as an editor, but she travels to New York like every three weeks to go to meetings. She gets home tomorrow from another trip and I'm excited for her to come home. She's been gone almost a week this time and it gets weird not seeing her. Katie is my steady friend. She tends to keep me buttoned-down a little more.

Too much time away from her and I start getting the urge to do things that I know in my head are ridiculous but my heart thinks it would be fun.

Like painting my bedroom.

The rest of my house is this boring, normal color between gray and beige and while I do love the look of it, I'm in need of a little bit of pizazz in my house. So, I figured, I should just paint my bedroom something that will give me some energy when I wake up in the morning.

I like purple.

So purple it is.

The can of paint is already sitting in my garage, along with two brand new rollers and a couple of brushes.

It's going to be awesome.

Katie lives with my other dear friend, Ashten, and I can see her coming across the street as I am about to close the garage door. Probably should have put the paint out of sight. Ashten is not going to be a fan of the bright purple either.

"Eliza! Oh, Eliza!" She's waving at me, hurrying across the street and huffing as she comes into my garage. "Hi Eliza!" She's carrying a plate of Rice Krispy treats and smiling with this sort of fake-looking, cheesy grin.

Ashten is an elementary school teacher and I imagine that at the end of the day, she's just happy to see someone over the age of twelve who isn't making disgusting sounds with their armpits. But still. She's acting weird.

"Hey Ashten." I am trying to nonchalantly block the paint can with my purse, but my purse is small and in order to reach all the way down to the floor with it, I'm having to lean way over and slump one shoulder, so I imagine it's looking less nonchalant and more like I have disc issues in my upper back or I've been staring at the apes at our little town zoo for too long.

She doesn't comment on my Humpback of Norte Dame posture. "So, how was work? Did you care for all the mothers and babies?" Then she laughs this really odd laugh and I just look at her.

"What exactly is in those Rice Krispy treats?"

"These? Oh, just cereal, marshmallows and butter. I always follow the recipe *exactly*. I didn't follow it one time and I ended up with these nasty blobs of butter throughout the whole thing and a pan of soggy cereal."

She's super bubbly and Ashten, while she's normally very sweet and kind, is not super bubbly.

That can only mean one thing.

"Oh no."

She immediately snaps out of the cheesiness. "Now, before you get mad—"

"Too late."

"I mean, you did give him a key."

I rub my head. "Yes, but I gave it to him more just to satisfy him than for him to actually use it." I look around. "How did he even get here? Where's his car?"

Ashten shrugs. "It was here when I got home about four this afternoon," she says. "He must be out getting dinner or something."

Or he knew I would flip out when I got home and it was better to just let me adjust to the idea of him being here before he was actually in my house.

I bet he left his suitcase right in the middle of the living room so I'd see it and freak out while he was gone.

I sigh again.

"Sorry," Ashten says. She holds out the pan of Rice Krispies like an offering.

"I do love my brother, you know," I tell her, taking the bars.

"I know."

"He just doesn't let me do anything when he's around."

Last time he was in town, he wouldn't even let me run by Chick-fil-a on my way home for a frosted coffee after I got off work. It was too dark, drive-thrus are too dangerous and how could I even think of drinking something caffeinated at eight o'clock at night?

Ashten pats my shoulder. "I know."

"Well. Thanks for the dessert. Excuse me while I go eat the whole pan before he gets home." That way he can't make disapproving noises and shake his head all slowly every time I cut myself a square, then tell me how I'm overindulging in sugar and how that can lead to diabetes and heart failure and DEATH.

I am thirty-one years old. Surely I can feed myself, even if it is junk food. And if I perish, I perish.

Did Scarlett O'Hara say that? Or maybe it was a line from a junior-high performance of the Esther story? Either way, I don't appreciate when he starts telling me how to live my own life.

Ashten pats me again and leaves. I go inside and set the pan of Rice Krispy treats on the kitchen counter. The house is dark except for my living room lamp on the timer and Mike's suitcase is sitting there in the glow, right where I knew it would be.

The stink.

I'm finishing up my second square when I hear his key in the lock. I swivel on the barstool I'm sitting on and just watch as he comes in, smiling half-sheepishly, half happily at me.

"Hey Lyzie," he says.

"Mike."

He closes the door and locks it and then turns back to me, rubbing the back of his head. "Surprise."

"Uh, yeah. What are you doing here?" I'm honestly trying not to be exasperated, but this throws a huge kink into my plan to paint my pizzaz-y purple bedroom and then lay around in my pajamas and watch Disney princess movies until I have to go back to work again in four days.

"Well, you mentioned that you were off for a few days and you are rarely off on the weekends, so I just decided to come down and see you." He comes over and gives me a hug. "Make sure my little sister is doing okay."

Even as he's hugging me, I can see him looking around the kitchen, inspecting the ceiling and the floors.

The man is ridiculous.

"You have got to stop worrying about me," I tell him.

"It's my job."

"It's not your job."

He sighs. "Let's argue this later. What are you eating?"

I push the pan toward him. "Ashten brought over Rice Krispy treats."

"Ashten lives with Katie now?"

"Right."

He nods. I think Mike had a little thing for Katie a little bit ago but I don't know if anything ever came of it. Likely not. There have been approximately forty-three girls that I've thought Mike should ask out over the past fifteen years but nothing ever happens.

I look at my brother and down at my phone, checking the date. "Fourteenth," I tell him quietly and he nods.

"Yeah."

I think I know the reason Mike is here now.

Mom was only forty-two when she died of breast cancer, exactly fifteen years ago tomorrow. When I was little, forty-two sounded ancient. The older I get, the younger it sounds.

Mike shoves his hands in the front pockets of his jeans and leans back against my kitchen island. The kitchen was hands-down the biggest selling point of this particular house. Beautiful granite, upgraded cabinets, premium appliances. The rest of the house looked terrible in comparison when I moved in. I think it must have been a flip house in progress and whoever was flipping it ran out of money when they finished the kitchen. It worked out for me because I got a crazy good deal on it since it was only halfway done.

I've done a few things since I moved here but there's still a lot left to do. Like paint.

Mike looks tired. And in need of a haircut. I nod to the mop on top of his head.

"What, did Candace's scissors break?"

"She quit."

My mouth drops open. "No!"

"Yep. Said she couldn't trust her hands anymore because of the arthritis."

Candace has been our family stylist since before I was born, I'm pretty sure. She was one of those rare people who knew exactly how to style your hair so that the streak of neon blue you begged her to dye wasn't super obvious so you didn't get in trouble right away.

"Who is going to cut your hair now?" I ask. I found a new stylist here and she was pretty good. Probably a better stylist than Candace but not nearly as personable.

"Exactly why my hair looks like it does," Mike says, with a sigh.

For as much as I hate predictability, Mike exists on it.

"You could go to the girl I see here."

"Nah."

Ten bucks that's exactly what he said to himself when debating whether or not he should ask Katie out.

"So, why don't you ask Katie out?" I ask him.

He blinks at me. "What?"

"Katie. My friend Katie? Across the street Katie?"

He shakes his head. "That was a quick change of subject."

"I know you like her. Or at least, it seemed like you liked her."

He shrugs. "She's nice."

"Do you think she's pretty?"

He shrugs again which is Mike-speak for *yes*.

"So why haven't you ever asked her? I mean, you could even just ask her out to coffee or something."

Mike sighs. "I did ask her to coffee. We just never went. And I reminded her once about it and she kind of brushed it off."

"What? No!"

"I mean, not with quite that much enthusiasm, but yeah. That's basically how it went."

I roll my eyes. "You know what I meant. And seriously? I really thought there could have been something there."

"Well, apparently not."

"Katie's crazy. Just ask Ashten if Katie's crazy. Or Katie herself."

He smiles. "It was for the best. Long distance doesn't work well anyway. I mean, just look at you and Cooper."

I hold up my hands. "Whoa, whoa. Cooper and I were a *completely* different story. Completely. And it was not the long distance that broke us up. I ended it years ago."

"He said you stopped dating because you moved here."

"Cooper has never remembered the details about our relationship status very well," I say, rolling my eyes.

I remember one time I opened the front door and found him standing there with flowers for our two-year anniversary.

We only dated for like four months.

He's one of Mike's best friends though, so I kind of still put up with him. Honestly, it was nice to move here and not be constantly seeing him all the time. Change of scenery and all that.

"What exactly happened between you guys?" Mike asks me.

I shrug. "Nothing happened, we just weren't a good match," I tell him. "It wasn't anyone's fault. He just isn't the right guy."

The right guy will not be someone I've known since I was six hours old, I can guarantee that. I mean, we have pictures of Cooper and Mike sitting on our old 1970s style patchwork sofa as four year-olds holding me in their laps. And that's not even the worst. I think there's another picture of me in only a diaper holding Cooper's hand while we are eating popsicles on our old back porch.

If that doesn't scream *Little House on the Prairie* predictability, I don't know what does.

And we all know how I feel about that.

"Well, Coop won't give up."

"I pray every night that he will." Seriously. I get an email from him about once a week asking how I'm doing and telling me all about his life in St. Louis.

Mike grins. "There's a reason we've been friends so long."

"You're both ridiculously clingy? Is that why you are here?"

"Exactly." He rakes a hand through his hair and smiles gently at me. "No, I just didn't want you to be alone tomorrow."

I probably wouldn't have realized the date until I was going to bed, honestly. Especially considering how I was planning on painting the day away. Which means I would have just been crying in my room by myself.

Maybe it's good Mike came.

Fifteen years is a long time.

"Rice Krispy?" I offer him and amazingly, he accepts.

CHAPTER *Two*

I wake up to the smell of eggs.

So here's a random thing about me. I like eggs. I like scrambled eggs, hard-boiled eggs and eggs over hard.

I do not like any kind of eggs first thing in the morning.

The first thing I should be smelling in the morning is not something that came out of a chicken's tush, all scrambled and heated up.

I stumble out of bed, brush my teeth and walk into the kitchen, grimacing.

"Morning, Lyzie."

"What are you doing?"

"Making breakfast." He points to the pan and he's got enough eggs in the skillet for about five people.

"Are we expecting company?"

He looks at me. "Are we? I can make more eggs."

"How many did you make?"

"Well, I mean, I figured you'd have about two and I eat six."

"*Six*?" I am in shock and I don't shock very easily first thing in the morning before I've had my coffee. All pistons are not firing as sharply as they do after a few cups of caffeine. Pre-coffee, you could tell me that my new patient just delivered triplets from three different fathers, all with fifteen family members who all want to be in the room twenty-four hours a day and I would take it in stride. Post coffee, you could tell me a fly landed on my hair and I would spaz out like a head banger at a heavy metal concert.

Perhaps it's in the best interest of my patients for me to stop drinking coffee. But the drinking of coffee is what keeps the charts being completed and the names being remembered, so there's that to consider too.

Mike plates the eggs and sets one plate on the table at my spot. I gag as I turn on my Keurig and the water begins to heat up.

"What?"

"I hate eggs."

"They're good for you."

"So are pancakes."

"Pancakes are not good for you, Lyzie," Mike says, rolling his eyes.

"They are good for the heart." I brew a cup of French roast and set it on the table in front of Mike, all straight black and dark, without any hint of sweetness.

Sort of like his soul.

I kid. It's just the smell of the eggs talking.

Kind of kidding, anyway.

I dump a teaspoon of sugar into my coffee, stir in some cream and sit down at the table, pushing the eggs away.

"Let me pray," Mike says and then he just starts, nodding his head down and closing his eyes. "Jesus, we love you. We want to honor you with our lives and our hearts. Please protect us today and keep us safe. Please give Mom an extra big hug from us today. And please help Eliza to eat her eggs like a good girl. Amen."

I look at Mike and just shake my head. "Nope. Sorry."

"It was worth a shot."

"What do you want to do today?" I ask him.

"I'm the one who surprised you this weekend. What did you already have planned?" Mike asks, shaking an ungodly amount of pepper over his eggs.

"You know, if you have to use half the shaker of pepper to make the eggs palatable to eat, maybe you should just stick with pancakes," I say.

"Ah, but pancakes just stick with me." He pats the front of his stomach. "I'm not nineteen anymore with a nineteen year-old's metabolism, unfortunately."

I think back to when Mike was nineteen. I was fifteen and a sophomore in high school. I had braces, thick poofy hair that I couldn't keep de-frizzed, so I spent most of the time looking like a poodle with a bit in it's mouth.

Add to that my stellar fashion sense, and we are talking about a pretty horrific scene that should probably be erased from the pages of history.

Unfortunately, that would require me tracking down and burning the three hundred plus yearbooks holding those pictures. I'm not sure that's possible.

Though it could be.

Mike, on the other hand, skated through high school and college in like this golden glow. He was fit, he was tanned, he was born with the straightest teeth known to man. He was this huge football star and he and Cooper were the dream team of the entire school. Cooper, the all-star quarterback, and Mike, the all-star receiver. They were constantly together, like a right hand and a left hand.

And then there was me. The poodle who'd had a bad electrical shock.

We made quite the spectacle whenever we went out.

Sometimes I get extremely thankful that my adolescence took place before all these cell phone pictures and selfies and Facebook.

Dear goodness, what selfies have done to this world is just awful.

"I'm painting," I tell Mike.

"Great. I'll help you."

"Thanks, but no thanks." Mike is nothing less than annoying to work with when it comes to house projects. If it isn't done *exactly* to his liking, he gets this expression on his face and it just makes me nuts.

"What? I'm a great painter."

"I know."

"So why don't you want my help?"

"Because you will make me go buy that blue tape stuff and I don't want to buy it. It's expensive and it makes me crazy ripping it back up off the baseboards."

"You'd rather have drips all over the baseboards? What color are you painting anyway? And what room?"

"Purple and my room."

Mike chokes on an egg. "Seriously, Lyzie? Purple?"

"It's my room."

"Yeah, but aren't you worried that you'll start dreaming about Barney or something every night if you fall asleep in a purple room?"

I grin.

"I can help you. I won't even make any comments about the lack of properly preparing your space."

"Fine."

"Fine." He smiles all self-sufficiently. "When do you want to start?"

"Soon. The paint fumes can cover up the smell of those nasty eggs."

"Since when did you start hating eggs? You always liked eggs."

"I like them after eleven o'clock."

Mike just shakes his head.

We get breakfast cleaned up and we are in my room a little bit later, laying down trash bags over the carpet so I can set the paint can down. I shake it up a little bit, pop it open and use one of the wooden stir sticks to smooth it all around.

"Wow."

"Don't say it."

"That paint is purple." Mike's eyes are wide. "Like if purple married purple and they had a purple baby. What's the brand? Willy Wonka?"

"You can leave."

"I won't say anything else."

I pour some paint into a tray, grab my roller and get to work. The first roll onto the wall and I start having some doubts, but goodness knows I'm not going to say a word of those doubts to Mike, since he's standing there, arms crossed over his chest, shaking his head.

So, maybe I'll repaint in a few weeks. Who cares? Paint is relatively cheap.

"Sure about this, Lyzie?"

I've got like a four-by-four foot square on the wall and I think the paint is getting more neon the longer I look at it.

So, maybe I look ridiculous to Mike. There is no way I can rest properly in a neon purple bedroom.

"I don't think they gave me the right color," I say, looking at the paint can. "The paint color card had a lot more of a bluish-purple tone to it."

"That's neon," Mike points out, like I have been blinded and can't see thanks to the square on my wall.

"Yeah, I've noticed."

"So, what do you want to do? I don't think you can take back paint that has already been colored."

I sigh and put the top back on the paint. "What a waste."

"Do you have more of this color?" Mike asks, nodding to the original grayish-beige of my room.

"It's in the garage."

He leaves and returns a few minutes later with the can and a new sleeve for my roller, along with a roll of paper towels. "Here," he says and takes my purple-coated roller. He pulls the sleeve off with the paper towels and puts the new, clean sleeve on the roller, passing it back over. He sets the roller in the paint tray and hands me a clean tray.

"Might want to let it dry a little bit first," he says.

"Probably." I sigh. "That's sad. I was looking forward to a purple bedroom."

"No, you really weren't. You just like change."

"There's that too."

He shakes his head. "I've never understood that about you."

"I know."

He takes the purple paint away and I do a few things in my room while I wait for it to dry on the wall. Mike never comes back so I go looking for him and find the bottom half of him coming out of my kitchen cabinets.

"Mike?"

"Yeah?" His voice is all echo-y inside the cabinet, under my sink.

"What are you doing?"

"Checking to make sure you aren't at risk for any leaks from your disposal."

I look at the sink for a minute. "Did you see a leak or was it making a weird sound or something?"

"Nope."

"So you're worried about this because...?"

"Because it happens and I don't want you to come out here one morning and find a pond where your kitchen is supposed to be."

I look at the floor, at the sink and back at Mike's legs sticking out of the cabinet. "Hey Mike?"

"Yeah?"

"My disposal is fine."

"That's what our old neighbors said right before they started growing algae on their kitchen floor. Took them six months to get all the damaged fixed."

"I do not remember this happening to any of our neighbors."

"You were little. I'm sure you don't. Plus, you were too busy playing My Little Pony in the backyard to notice Coop and me dragging the damaged tile and cabinets out of the kitchen."

"I'm not that much younger than you, Mike. Surely if you were old enough to be doing that, I was old enough to not be playing My Little Pony." I frown. "And anyway, I don't think I ever even had a My Little Pony. Mom thought they were demonic."

Mike sticks his head out of the cabinet and grins at me. "Mom did not think they were demonic."

"Sure she did. She said that they were right along the same lines as Care Bears. And I know she thought those were demonic."

"She did not! She thought they were ridiculously expensive for what was basically a cheaply made, neon-colored teddy bear." He comes out from under the sink and puts the box of trash bags and my kitchen cleaner back under there, closing the door.

"Hey Mike?"

"Yeah?"

I rub my cheek. "Do you ever wonder if maybe Dad hadn't died in the wreck Mom would have tried a little harder to live?"

Mike's face goes from smiling to creased and lined like he's aged about ten years in the ten seconds it took me to ask the question.

"Eliza," he says, drawing my name out. He sighs and just reaches over and pulls me into a hug. "It's just best not to wonder," he says, squeezing my shoulders. "We just need to not wonder."

As far as I can tell, this means yes.

CHAPTER *Three*

Hey! Any chance you can pick me up from the airport in about two hours? Ashten just found out she has to take a shift at Minnie's.

I see Katie's text at three o'clock that afternoon. I'm half tempted to just send Mike over to the airport to pick her up.

Which airport? I write back. Sometimes Katie flies back into St. Louis and just drives back, but sometimes she takes a little puddle hopper from St. Louis back here to Carrington Springs. We don't have a big airport, but they have the space for some of those little tiny flyers that make you think about scheduling a time to meet with your life insurance agent before you fly.

Carrington Springs.

It only takes about twenty minutes to pick her up and get back home. I shrug. *Sure.*

Now the question. Do I send Mike? Or is that just awkward and could ruin my friendship with Katie?

"What's up?" Mike is coming inside from where he was mowing my backyard for me. Not that it needed it. It's barely starting to turn green out there.

"Katie needs a ride from the Carrington Springs airport," I tell him.

Mike nods. "Okay. What time?"

"About five."

"Why don't you go get her and after you're done, we can go out to eat? I'll get showered while you're gone."

I nod to his unspoken request to not see Katie. "Good. I wasn't going to say anything but a shower would be good."

"You're mean."

"You smell terrible."

"That's because I've been working."

Sometimes I think Mike works so hard so he doesn't have to think about things. Especially on a day like today when memories are thick and the void feels very long and deep and wide.

Neither of my parents even knew that I wanted to be a nurse.

It's such a huge part of my identity now. And them not knowing just makes it seem like even longer since they were here.

"Okay," I say, rather than bring up the discussion. It's not the time. I was sixteen when Mom died and I miss her terribly and a part of me always will. But I didn't feel the weight of a sibling to finish raising like Mike did.

I leave for the airport at four-forty and Katie is tossing her suitcase into my trunk into my car thirty minutes later.

"Hey," I say, smiling at her as she opens the passenger door.

Katie is obviously exhausted. She falls into the seat and smiles wearily at me, rubbing her messy bun. "Hey. Thanks so much for picking me up, Eliza. I hope you didn't have plans."

I wave a hand as I pull out of the pick up lane. "Not really. Mike surprised me and came into town this weekend, but we weren't doing anything. He's trying to redo my entire backyard, but other than that, we're just hanging out."

"Oh Eliza, I would have never asked you if I knew Mike was in town!"

"It's really fine, Katie."

"Sure I didn't mess up plans?"

"Promise. Mike is showering and we're going to dinner when I get back." I look over at her. "You can join us if you want."

"Thanks. I think I'll pass today. I'm so tired. I never sleep good in hotels. I might just go pick up a broccoli cheese soup at Panera and call it a night."

I nod. "Makes sense."

"Thanks though."

"Sure. No problem. Bible study at your house on Wednesday, right?"

Soon after I first met Katie, we started doing a little Bible study at her house. It started with just the two of us, Ashten and a few random people I invited from work and now it's grown into this huge thing. Every week, we've had between fifteen and thirty people coming consistently. I think one time I counted forty-five and poor Katie was about to lose her mind. I mean, I kind of understood. Forty-five people are way too many to have crammed into the living room and kitchen of your own home.

We've talked about maybe moving it to someplace bigger but I'm just not sure where we will go. The whole point of the Bible study being in our houses is that it wasn't tied to a church and it was a lot less threatening to invite people who weren't Christians then. Somehow, it's a lot easier to say, "Hey, come to my friend Katie's house and eat all her chocolate chip cookies" than to say, "Come to my church and get preached to."

I don't know.

Katie is nodding though. We went through First John and now we are about to start James.

Honestly, I'm a little scared of James. He's big into actions. I'm big into words.

It's what I do best.

"I tried my best to prep as much as I could while I was in between meetings," Katie says.

"Hey, did you see that guy?"

"What guy? I saw lots of guys."

"The guy that your coworker set you up with awhile ago? Jason? Mason? Grayson?"

Katie grins at me. "Justin."

"Oh right." I have to memorize too many names at work to remember names outside of the hospital. "So did you see him?"

She shakes her head. "No, I didn't even tell him I was in town, actually."

I nod. "Good choice."

There's a lot that I love about Katie. She's super kind, she's got this gentle sense of humor that isn't sarcastic and she loves Jesus. That being said, she's kind and gentle and sometimes I've noticed that it can be a bad thing in her life. She's wanted to get married for like ten years and I'm just worried that she's going to kindly and gently work her way into a marriage that resembles more of a Mr. Collins and Charlotte thing than a Mr. Darcy and Elizabeth thing.

And I, as resident best friend and across the street neighbor, refuse to let that happen.

Besides, I would really like it if she married my brother so we could just be sisters and done with it. We could spend every Christmas together then.

And trust me, I am a great person to have around during the holidays.

"So, where does that stand?" I ask.

"Where does what stand? Justin?"

I wave a hand. "Sure. Justin. Men. Whoever. What's going on? I haven't talked to you in a long time."

Katie sighs and melts into my passenger seat, rubbing her eyes. "I don't even know."

"Well, I happen to know of a lonely and fairly attractive guy who is currently so lonely and attractive that he's crashing my weekend off."

Katie smiles over at me. "I like Mike, I really do."

"There's a *but* coming."

"But – "

"There it is."

She rolls her eyes at me. "But, I just don't think that our personalities click."

"Did you give him a personality test or something? Mike is weird, don't get me wrong, but he'll take care of you. Probably more than you want to be cared for."

She grins. "Oh I know. That's why it probably won't work."

I look over at her and the way she's picking at a hangnail on her right hand.

She's not telling me something. I know her too well. We've only been friends for a fairly short amount of time, but I can read Katie like a just-released hardcover.

I remember a while ago, she was all nervous and pink-cheeked around a guy who worked as a wedding singer. Luke something. We go to the same church. He often sits by us and maybe it's because of my kind and gentle friend.

Time for a stakeout.

We get back to our street and I park in my driveway. "Hope you sleep well," I tell her as she gets her suitcase out.

"Thanks, Eliza. And thanks for the ride." She yanks the handle up and gives me a hug, rolling her suitcase across the street. "Love you!" she hollers behind her.

"Love you back." I go inside and Mike is standing in the kitchen, reading a paper.

I frown. "Where did you get that? 1998?"

"Hardy-har-har. For your information, I actually enjoy reading the paper. I picked it up on my way into town yesterday."

"So it's not just old news, it's obsolete news?"

He looks at me over the paper. "You forget that I was going to pay for dinner tonight."

"Enjoy your reading."

"Thank you." He sets the paper down. "Where would you like to go?"

I know where I would like to go but I'm worried that if I'm right, it will make Mike feel bad.

"So are you pretty much over the whole Katie thing working out?" I ask him.

He shakes his head, sighing. "Liza," he starts.

I hold up a hand to interrupt. "No, I'm not trying to set you guys up. I just think she might be interested in someone and I think she's potentially meeting him for dinner tonight but just doesn't want to tell me. So, if you're totally over her, I thought maybe we could go spy on her. But if you're not, then I'm fine going somewhere else."

"Oh Lyzie."

"So is that a yes?"

He just laughs and then knuckles my head.

Panera is not crowded this time of night.

I think it's more of a lunch place. At least, I hope it is. I rarely come here but if this is any indication of the type of crowds they keep, then I guess it's good that I'm not addicted to them like Katie is. She's going to be sad when they close because of they have no business.

We order our food and sit down in one of the corners. I made sure that Katie's car was still in her driveway before we left so we got here first. And I ordered a broccoli cheese soup. Katie always talks about it and I've never gotten it before. I'm not a huge fan of broccoli. I

41

do like cheese but cheese soup has always flirted a little closely with the line between dip and fondue, so we will see how this goes.

Mike ordered some multi-meat sandwich with no bun and they set the sad plate in front of him and he's immediately grousing about it.

"It's like food made for gerbils," he says.

"It's because you didn't order a bun," I tell him. "It is food for gerbils."

"Not the ingredients. The amount of ingredients." He waves his hand at his plate. "This is not enough food for a fully-grown human being. This is barely enough food for a guinea pig. And it cost what? Like twelve dollars?" He's shaking his head. "No wonder there is no one here."

"All right, we can keep it down now." I'm sounding an awful lot like Cogsworth all of a sudden and I sort of want to burst into *Be Our Guest* but that doesn't really fit my M.O. of blending into the corner booth so we can be spying on Katie tonight.

Ten minutes later, in walks Katie.

Alone.

I quietly gnaw on the top of my bread bowl and squish farther down in the seat. Maybe I was wrong? She steps up to the register and I smile to myself.

"What?" Mike asks, looking at me and then back at Katie. "She's not with the guy."

"Yeah, but she put on makeup."

"So?"

"So, Katie doesn't put on makeup if she's just coming to sit by herself."

He nods. "Got it."

Sure enough, about three minutes later, a taller guy with crazy curly hair, glasses and a five o'clock shadow walks in and Katie grins over at him.

Well, well.

"Who's that?" Mike whispers to me.

"Luke Brantley," I tell him.

So, Katie likes Luke. I sit back in the booth and nod to myself. I mean, she could do a lot worse. Luke is funny. He's a consultant or something during the week and a wedding singer on the weekends. I've heard him sing. He sounds like Michael Buble.

So I mean, good for her.

"Well, I was right. We can go home now."

Mike grins. "You don't want to keep watching?"

I shrug. "They're just going to eat and talk. And as much fun as that is to watch, I'm okay missing it."

Mike finishes his rodent food and nods. "Sounds good. Let's not ever come here again."

"Not a fan?"

"They need to up the doses over here. I paid sixteen dollars for this and I'm still starving."

I grin. "I'm pretty sure it wasn't sixteen dollars."

"The hunger is messing with my head."

"Order bread next time, weirdo."

We get back home and Mike unearths a container of popcorn kernels out of the depths of my pantry.

I swear I have never seen the container before. "Where did you get that?" I ask, frowning.

"I bought it last time I was here."

"What is it?"

"Popcorn."

I look at it. "No, it's not."

"Eliza. It's popcorn. It's what popcorn looks like before it gets popped."

"How do you pop it without the envelope thing?"

"The envelope full of artificial ingredients?"

"And butter flavoring."

"Dear goodness, I have taught you nothing. It's amazing that you can even survive out here without me. Sure you don't want to move back to St. Louis?"

I smile at him, hearing the real question behind the joking. "I'm happy here, Mike. I really am."

"I know. I just…" He shrugs and pulls out my larger saucepan. "I miss you, kid."

"I miss you, too."

"Well, there's a nice house for sale right by my apartment."

"I already own a house. But thank you."

"Coop would be thrilled if you moved back."

I roll my eyes. "Cooper needs to just get over it and move on with life."

"Right," Mike scoffs. "Like that will happen. Pass me the coconut oil."

"I don't think I have any."

"It's in the back of your pantry next to the unsalted almonds."

I find a jar of coconut oil and look at the nice little assortment of foods that I do not remember ever purchasing. "Glad to see you've made yourself at home," I tell him, handing him the jar.

Mike grins. "I just buy a little each time I come. And look, you haven't even noticed."

I watch him melt the coconut oil down and add in a few kernels of popcorn. Once they pop, he pours in about a third cup of kernels, covers the saucepan and starts shaking it over my stove.

"So."

"So."

Mike looks over at me while he's shaking the saucepan. "I brought it with me."

I was wondering. Our evening plans are set. I nod and pull out my biggest mixing bowl for him to pour the hot popcorn into. "So, where is the butter flavoring?" I ask him.

"No butter flavoring. Coconut oil is way better for you."

"You're killing me, Smalls."

Mike grins at the reference. "Really, though, I'm helping you live longer. Okay. Salt?"

I hand him the salt shaker and he carries the bowl into the family room a minute later, reaching over to pull a DVD off the sofa.

He hands it to me, I put it in the DVD player and join him on the couch with the remote.

Two year-old me is grinning shyly from the TV a minute later. "Lyzie, Lyzie-girl, sing your song!" Mom is saying and I start singing "The Wheels on the Bus" in a barely audible voice.

"Louder, Liza," my dad says from behind the camera. "I can't hear you."

"Here, just let me sing it," six year-old Mike pushes in front of the camera. *"The wheels on the bus—"*

"No! It's my turn!"

"Michael and Eliza." Mom's got her I-mean-business voice on now. You can hear Dad quietly sniffing a laugh behind the camera.

Mike grins over at me, getting himself a handful of popcorn. "Twenty-nine years later and just as squealy."

"Please. Twenty-nine years later and just as bossy."

We watch quietly as Mom gives us both hugs and then runs her hand through our hair like she always did. Even on her last day, the last time I hugged her before she died, she still ran her fingers through my hair and tucked it behind my ear.

And suddenly, I can't stop the tears.

CHAPTER *Four*

I show up for work on Tuesday feeling a little ragged around the edges. I don't often get four days off in a row and it's always like going to back to work after Christmas break to walk back into the hospital when my break is over.

I close my purse inside my locker and rub my eyes. It's 6:45am.

Mftph.

I'd almost rather just get two days off in a row. I'm not responsible enough to continue to go to bed at a decent time during a four-day break. Which just means that I'm dragging my whole first day back.

"How was your weekend?" April, one of my coworkers puts her purse in her locker and smiles at me, adjusting her badge on her lanyard.

"Good. My brother surprised me and came into town."

"That's fun!"

I nod. "It was fun. I'm so tired though now."

"I bet. I feel like having company stay with you is a little like making a chocolate soufflé. The end result is nice and you're left with this happy glow, but process of getting to that happy glow is just a lot of hard work and exhaustion."

I laugh. "Right."

"Speaking of exhaustion, I saw Tara from the night shift and we've got two sets of twins today."

"Joy." Somehow, I always end up with the twins. Not that I mind it, but it just takes me that much longer to get through my rounds.

I remember wishing I was a twin when I was about eleven or so and maybe twins would be fun about that age. But any younger would just be miserable. Two crying babies, two teething toddlers, two potty-training at the same time?

It sounds awful.

But there are days that I leave work thinking one baby just sounds awful, so maybe I'm not the best judge here.

I get my assignments, make my initial rounds with the night shift nurse, mark down my notes and the day begins.

Three moms, four babies. I run from room to room, checking fundal heights and catheters, changing out pads and sheets, bathing babies and teaching terrified fathers how to change diapers.

I almost had to have one poor dad breathe into a paper sack first.

Sort of ridiculous considering the labor and delivery his wife just went through, but still. I kind of felt sorry for the guy.

Seven o'clock comes quickly and slowly at the same time and suddenly, I'm clocking out, blocking a yawn with my elbow.

"Another four-day weekend for you, huh?"

"Yeah, it was nice but kind of long." I smile at Tara, the night nurse.

"No, I mean, you've got another one coming up. What are you going to do this time?"

I check the schedule and shake my head. "I mean, those are great and all, but I start getting bored."

Tara rolls her eyes. "You can borrow my kids, if you want."

I grin. "No thanks." Tara has a thirteen year-old and a seventeen year-old. If there's any better birth control than working around freshly postpartum women, it's listening to the stories that moms of teens have.

I get home and Katie's lights are on, Ashten's car is out front.

So, I park in my garage and walk on over, knocking on the front door. Ashten opens the door a second later.

"Didn't we give you a key?" she asks me.

"It's in my house. I didn't walk all the way in."

Ashten grins. "I can tell. Nice puppies." She nods to my scrub pants.

"Thanks. I wear it for the kids."

"Aren't the kids you work with barely able to see more than eight inches?"

"Beside the point," I say, waving my hand.

She smiles. "What are you up to tonight? Katie put chicken in the crock pot. Want some?"

This is the best perk of having your best friends live across the street. If I'm off, I cook. When Katie's working, she's at home and she cooks. We just kind of share every meal and it's basically the best thing ever.

"Sure," I say, smiling. "I've got cookies at my house that I can run go get."

"What kind?" Ashten asks warily.

"Good grief. I experiment one time and now it's like every time I bake, I get questioned like I used cyanide in the last batch."

"I don't care what Pinterest says, you don't put chili powder in cookies."

"They were supposed to be like a spicy sweet thing."

"That only works in Chinese food and notice that the Chinese are not known for their chocolate chip cookies."

I grin.

Katie comes down the hall wearing her work clothes, which are always yoga pants and a long tank top. Tonight, she's got an oversized sweatshirt jacket on top, hands buried in the pockets.

She looks adorable but Katie always looks adorable.

I have a hard time understanding why she's still not married, especially considering her desire to be. She hasn't even really been in a long-term relationship. It's just bizarre.

I know Ashten was in a serious relationship a little while ago but nothing super recently. She's too sweet to be single for long.

And then there's me. I fully intend on waiting it out. I feel like looking for the right guy is similar to shopping for used cars. Some cars look great on the outside, but they have that fake pleather stuff on the inside that smells weird when the car has been sitting in the sun for too long. Some cars have super plush interiors, but the outsides are all scraped up. Some cars are purely for walking outside and just looking at them in the garage but never taking them on the road.

I'll put it like this. Mr. Darcy doesn't come along every day.

So, I'll wait. I know for a fact that I haven't already met him. And the odds are good that I won't meet him at work, sad to say. All the doctors on my floor are happily married, so we can all put our *Grey's Anatomy*-clouded imaginations aside.

"Dude," I say.

Katie shakes her head. "That's dudette to you. How was work? You look like you just got off at the pound."

"Hey, the doggies are the kids' favorite."

"Please."

"I always have way less tears when I wear these pants."

"From the babies or the mothers?" Ashten grins, settling on one of the kitchen barstools.

"Both."

"Right," Katie says. She goes over to the crockpot and opens the lid, the smell of chicken wafting out.

I know a lot of people who genuinely enjoy the smell of chicken cooking and tell me how it smells like home and whatever. I just don't like it. I enjoy eating chicken. Chicken salad made like my mom used to make it with grapes and sugared pecans might be one of my favorite dishes in the world.

But I don't have to enjoy smelling it beforehand.

"What did you make?" I ask.

"Barbecue chicken," Katie says. "Ash, there's buns in the pantry, if you want to grab those."

Katie shreds the chicken in the crockpot, douses it with more barbecue sauce and then pulls a tray of sweet potato fries from the oven. "One of these days, I'm getting myself a fryer," she declares.

"Please don't. I will double my weight in a year," I tell her.

"You don't have to eat the fried food."

"Are you kidding me? You think I'll just sit over there by myself while you guys are making homemade donuts and fries and cronuts and whatever else? Oreos?"

Katie sets the tray on a hot pad and turns to me. "First off, cronuts sound amazing. What are they?"

"Croissants that are fried like donuts."

"Dear goodness."

"Exactly."

"And second off," Katie continues, back to her stern voice. "I will never fry an Oreo. Ever."

"Good girl," Ashten nods. "And I am in favor of adding a fryer to this house."

"I won't be able to fit into my puppy scrubs," I say.

"That is not necessarily a bad thing," Katie grins.

"Meany."

"What else can I get, Katie?"

"There's fruit salad in the fridge." She reaches back into the oven and pulls out foil-wrapped ears of corn and sets them on a big plate.

I stopped commenting on the feasts at Katie's house long ago. She always claims that I make a lot of food for them, and maybe I do, but she's just as guilty as me.

Besides, I'm a big fan of leftovers. The more leftovers, the happier I am. My mother always told me that a happy fridge was one that was on the verge of an old-fashioned shepherd's pie.

I never completely understood why they call it pie.

Sort of sullies the good name of pie, in my opinion.

We sit down at the table with full plates a few minutes later and Ashten blesses the food. "Thank you for the food, thank you for the hands that prepared it and thank you for these dear sisters. Amen."

Ashten's prayers are always short and sweet. Sort of like her.

"So, how was it going back to work today?" Katie asks me.

I moan. "Horrible. And I found out that I have another four day weekend this coming week."

"You are the only person I know who complains about days off," Ashten says, taking a bite of her sandwich.

"I don't mind the days off. I just get bored. And then I get into the habit of staying up until two in the morning and sleeping until ten and then I can barely get to work on time when it's time to go back."

"What do you even do at two in the morning?" Katie asks, shaking her head.

Katie and Ashten are both very similar in their bedtime habits, which probably makes them very compatible as roommates. They are always, without fail, regardless of the day of the week, in bed by no later than eleven and they are always up by seven, if not earlier.

Even on Saturdays.

They are just weird.

If I don't have a reason to get up, I don't get up.

I shrug to Katie's question. "I don't know. I read. I watch movies. Sometimes I work on stuff around the house."

There's something strangely energizing about being the only person awake in the neighborhood.

Katie shakes her head. "I just don't get it. Anyway. So what are you going to do next weekend?"

"I don't know."

"You should go surprise Mike. See how well he likes it."

"He'd probably have me settled in an apartment before the end of the four days."

Ashten grins. "Probably."

I haven't been back to St. Louis since I left. Mike's always come here. Part of me is worried to go back, like maybe I'll suddenly realize I've been terribly homesick this whole time and I'll transfer back to the hospital there before I even think about it.

Then there's this whole other part of me that's worried if I go back, I won't miss it at all.

Considering everything that happened in St. Louis, I don't know which one is worse.

The thought of visiting, though, sounds kind of nice. I nod, chewing my sandwich. "Maybe I will do that," I say.

"You should," Ashten says. "It would be good for you."

"Are you working at the restaurant this summer?" I ask Ashten and she starts nodding.

"Yep. Every summer."

Ashten is a teacher but when she's not teaching, she waitresses at her family's amazing restaurant, Minnie's Diner. Minnie's is like a Carrington Springs legend. People drive all the way from St. Louis just for the rolls. The place is gigantic and more often than not, half of the huge parking lot is filled with luxury tour buses from all those places that do those drive across the country trips for seniors.

Someday, when I am old, I will not ride on a bus to see the country, regardless of how luxurious the bus is or how beautiful the purple mountain majesties look from the bus window.

I can get motion sickness just stirring my coffee in the morning, so it's probably best to stay off the bus.

"Do they pay you to work there?" Katie asks. "Or is it some like 'you have the privilege of working for the family' type of a thing?"

Ashten grins. "Yeah, as much as I love my family, I'm pretty sure I'm too old to work for free. That being said, I did give them at least six summers of work without pay."

"You should ask for back pay," Katie says.

"And see if they'll pay you in rolls," I add.

"You who are all concerned about your puppy pants still fitting," Katie says.

I laugh.

CHAPTER *Five*

Considering the rest of Missouri, St. Louis is a gigantic city. It's a big city regardless, but now that I'm used to tiny Carrington Springs, it just feels monstrous.

I drive the familiar roads to Mike's apartment. When Dad died in the car accident, Mom decided to sell the house we had grown up in and move to an apartment. At the time, she kept saying how the memories were just too hard and she just couldn't handle constantly feeling like Dad was going to walk in the door at any moment.

Now, though, I wonder if she knew she was sick and she just couldn't bear the thought of Mike and I having to deal with the house too.

When she died, we really didn't have that much to do as far as tying up Mom's affairs. We stayed in the same apartment, I stayed in my same bedroom. After I moved to Carrington Springs, Mike just stayed where he was.

I park out front and climb the stairs to the apartment. It's Thursday about four o'clock and I know Mike is still at work. He'll have to work tomorrow too, so I brought some shopping money with me. I'm going to try and find some new bedding for my room. I've had the same comforter since middle school and when I washed it last time, the batting inside it got all lumpy.

It's probably time for a new one.

I unlock the door with my key and step inside.

Nothing has changed.

Like literally, nothing has changed. Even down to where the coffee table is positioned in front of the couch.

I rearrange my furniture approximately once a month just for it to look slightly different. I love the feeling of waking up the next morning and everything looking so new and changed.

Mike has never been that way. One time I moved where Mom always kept the coffeepot over to under the cabinet where the coffee cups were because that just made a lot more sense to me. Mike had flipped out.

"You can't just change things!" he'd said, getting as close to yelling at me as he ever got. "Especially without talking to me first!"

After that, I never touched anything ever again. And Mike never got that mad at me ever again.

Looking around this apartment though, I wonder if Mike is doing okay. I mean, he almost had a fit when I moved to Carrington Springs.

I need change. I need things to be different. I need to experience new things and people and places. Too little change and I start feeling moldy.

"Well, well, well," Mike says, opening the door and grinning at me. "Look who missed her big brother."

"Hi Mike."

"I was hoping that was your car out there." He comes over and gives me a big hug. "What's with the visit? Didn't I just see you last weekend?"

I sigh. "I'm on another four day break and Ashten and Katie suggested I come here."

"Probably so you wouldn't bug them with all your sadness over not having to work."

I grin. "Probably." I had considered going on a little trip somewhere by myself but Mike would have flipped out if he ever found out. And besides, traveling alone is never fun. It always sounds fun until you're doing it and then it's just lonely.

All those people who post those selfies of them on the beach staring off into the distance having "time with their thoughts" must be so sad. I always lose a little bit of faith in humanity when I see those posts.

"Want to get tacos?" I ask Mike. "Or did you have dinner plans?"

He shakes his head. "No dinner plans. I brought some work home, but I don't need to do it. I do have to work tomorrow though."

"I figured. I'm going shopping. Carrington Springs didn't have any comforters I liked."

"You're changing your room again?"

"You say that like I change it every week. I was eleven when I got the comforter I have right now."

"I still have the same comforter I had when I was eleven."

I nod. "That's great. Mine is falling apart though."

"Mine probably is too but I think I'll hold on to it just a little longer."

I pray a lot for Mike's future wife. The man can get attached to a broken coat hanger.

"Let's go eat," I say. We need to leave before I'm tempted to just redecorate the entire apartment and push Mike out of his comfort zone.

This cannot be healthy.

We take Mike's car to one of the local taco places in town. These were Dad's favorites. The man had Scottish blood running through his veins but he loved tacos with all of his heart. I always joked with him that he had settled in the wrong state. Missouri isn't exactly known for it's Mexican food.

This particular restaurant is my favorite because there is a patio out front. We get our tacos and take them outside, watching the cars drive by and talking about nothing in particular.

Sometimes I do miss living close to Mike. It was just us for so long that it just feels normal for it to just be us again.

We go home and watch a movie. Mike has an early morning meeting, so he's in bed with the lights off by ten. I read for a little bit and then turn the light off in my room as well. This is the only room that has changed in this entire apartment and it's because I took most of my stuff with me.

I look at the ceiling that I stared at for so many years every single night and I'm asleep before I even realize I've closed my eyes.

Quilt shopping is the worst.

It's worse than bras. And very little is worse than bra shopping.

I rub my eyes and look at the choices that one of the home furnishings stores has in the St. Louis Galleria mall. Apparently, navy blue is in.

There's like eight navy blue comforters and quilts.

I'm not sure how I feel about navy. Is it cute in a sailor-ish kind of way? Does it have the same feeling as Sperry shoes and gold jewelry? Or is just a way for us to bring back the 90s because we are out of original ideas?

I pass on the quilts and move on to the next store. I've been shopping since ten o'clock this morning and it's now one and I'm starving. The Galleria has so many great restaurants, especially compared to the Carrington Springs' mall, so I walk over to a map to figure out what I want to eat.

My phone buzzes in a text and it's Mike.

Where are you?

He's already asked me this once about an hour ago. Typical Mike. He got better over the years, but especially right after Dad's accident, he was texting me about every thirty minutes to make sure I was okay.

Still at the Galleria. About to get lunch.

The Cheesecake Factory has a restaurant on the lower level here. I used to come here every other week with some girls from work before I moved.

That sounds good.

Where are you going to eat?

Cheesecake Factory.

I'll think of you while I eat my plain chicken over spinach.

I grin. Mike definitely got more of the Wakeman genes. That side of the family isn't necessarily the smallest. So I know he worries a lot about his weight but it's the reason that he is in such good shape. All of the men on my dad's side of the family are really large. My uncle has to be over three hundred pounds.

I know it scares Mike to death. Possibly even more than carbs.

I go downstairs to the restaurant and it's pretty crowded, even for one o'clock. "Just one," I tell the hostess loudly over the noise.

"Okay. Inside, patio or first available?"

"Patio please."

"It will be about ten minutes."

I guess it just looks crowded. I take my buzzer and go stand by the glass case displaying all the cheesecakes and try not to drip drool on it.

My buzzer goes off before ten minutes are up and I hand it to the waitress and follow her outside, finally breathing when I get outdoors. It's not that I don't like crowds, I honestly don't mind them. But I'm not a huge fan of the noise level in a lot of restaurants. I feel like you can't even hear yourself think.

If there's going to be loud volume, I like it to be me, not the table next to me.

I sit down and the waiter comes by a minute later with this half-pitied look on his face as he looks at the empty chair across from me at the two-person table. "Welcome to Cheesecake Factory," he says. "Can I get you a drink? Our alcoholic beverages are on the first two pages."

Apparently, since I am alone, I also want to drink my loneliness away.

I've kind of gotten used to eating alone, so I'm fine. I have my phone and a Kindle app. I'm going to read during lunch. Or people watch. Another reason to sit outside. "I'll take an iced tea," I say and he nods.

"I'll be right back with that."

I take a deep breath and slip my sunglasses on, looking out at the parking lot. It's a beautiful day in St. Louis. Humidity is low, sunshine is high and I am about to eat some form of chocolate cheesecake.

Regardless of my lack of success in finding a comforter, it's a great day.

"Eliza Lorraine Wakeman."

I look over which is silly because I already know who is standing behind me even before I turn all the way around.

"Cooper Grayson McClowski." I shake my head and pull my sunglasses off. "And how exactly did you know I would be here?"

Cooper grins his perfect grin and holds up his cell phone, reading out loud from the screen. "'She's eating lunch at the Cheesecake Factory by herself. Probably outside.'"

"Mike."

"Yep." He shoves his phone back into his pocket. "Well. Do I at least get a nice hello?"

I let my breath out in a sigh, but honestly, it is actually good to see Cooper. He was there for most of my childhood and really, he's still around in a lot of ways. He sends me an email at least once a week. Sometimes, he doesn't even propose in it.

Occasionally, anyway.

So I stand up and give him a hug. Cooper always has the best hugs. Maybe it's the big shoulders, I'm not sure.

"Well," he says, pushing me back to arm's length. "Glad to see that Carrington Springs has been good to you." He gives me a look, tipping his head down. "You happy?"

I nod. Rarely am I super successful with an impulse decision, which is basically what moving to Carrington Springs was, but this time it really did work out. "I am," I tell him. "I'm very happy."

"Good." He nods to the extra chair. "I'm starving. Let's eat."

"I assume you are joining my table," I say, rolling my eyes.

"Yep."

"So much for my quiet lunch of reading and people watching."

"Lyzie, I'm helping you out with that, see?" He sits and spreads his hands out wide. "I'm giving you a person to watch."

"Mm-hmm."

He grins. "I've missed you, kid."

"I know. Your emails remind me of that frequently."

"Can't blame a man for trying."

"No, but you can probably blame him for never giving up."

"My dad likes to say that it's the McClowski way," Cooper says, nodding. "'Never give up, never surrender.'"

"I'm pretty sure that's a line from *Galaxy Quest*. Not from something your father invented."

"Tim Allen stole it from Dad. Dad's been saying that since he was about six years old. And he probably got it from my grandfather, who was himself a stubborn McClowski man as well."

"Stubborn being the key word in all of this."

The waiter returns with my tea and is smiling all happily that I'm not sitting here alone anymore. "Hello!" he says with way too much enthusiasm to Cooper. "What can I get you to drink?"

"I'll take a root beer."

Gag. I make a face at Cooper and he smirks.

"Will do," the waiter makes a notation on his pad and looks at us. "Were you ready to order your meal as well? Can I start you with any appetizers? Crab cakes? Spinach and artichoke dip?"

"I'd like the blue cheese and pear flatbread," I order and the man nods.

"Excellent choice."

"Thank you."

"And for you, sir?"

"I'll have the orange chicken."

"Another excellent choice." The waiter puts his pen in his pocket and nods. "I'll be right back with some bread and that root beer, sir."

He leaves and Cooper looks across the table at me. "Still hate root beer, huh?"

"It smells like sadness."

Cooper laughs. "It smells like root beer. So. Tell me about Carrington Springs. Your emails aren't super informative."

"That's because contrary to you, I actually work for a living."

"Please. You work just as many shifts as I do in a week."

Cooper is a firefighter.

Growing up, he never wanted to play cops and robbers like Mike and I did, he wanted to pretend we were in a burning building and he had to come save us. So it was really no surprise when he said he wanted to become a firefighter. After Dad's accident, he was even more determined. The police investigator of the accident told us that if the EMTs had gotten there even five minutes earlier, Dad might have made it.

But it was rush hour and there was traffic and we had an EMT shortage and a million other reasons that all basically added up to it being God's timing for Dad to go home.

So, Cooper graduated from college and went straight to the fire academy.

"So?" he persists and I blink back to the conversation at hand.

"So, it's nice."

"As are a lot of places."

"It's got some really nice people who live there. My neighbors—"

"Katie and Ashten," Cooper interrupts.

"Right. My neighbors are great and I've really started liking the church I go to. It's just a nice small town but it's not so small that everyone knows everyone. And there's lots to do for it being so little."

"Which is why you are here on your time off." Cooper smirks at my expression and holds up his hands. "I'm just kidding! Sheesh, Lyzie. No, I'm glad you're doing so well there."

I gave him a look. "Really."

"Really. I am. I want you to be happy."

"Mm-hmm. So that forty-five minute talk the night before I left was just all for show?"

Cooper grins. "I didn't say *I* was happy. I just said I want you to be happy. I'm still not a fan of you being too far away for me to keep an eye on you."

"You sound like a stalker."

"Or a concerned party making sure that you are okay."

"Good grief. You and Mike are cut from the same cloth. After listening to you two, someone would think it was a miracle that I can tie my own shoes."

The waiter brings over our bread right then as Cooper laughs. "Some bread and here's your root beer. Anything else I can get you?"

"Do you have any type of iced coffee drinks?" I ask.

"I have iced coffee or several different types of espresso drinks that I can put over ice for you," he says.

"Great. I'll switch to iced coffee. And keep the refills coming."

He nods. "You got it."

Cooper grins at me. "Same old Eliza. Using caffeine to deal with me."

"It's honestly a medical marvel that my heart survived high school considering how much you were around."

"Sadly, mine didn't."

"Look, you've got to stop," I say, putting both hands on the table and leaning forward, lowering my voice.

"Lyzie."

"No, listen," I say, stopping his not-at-all-apologetic apology. "You always say stuff like that and maybe it was cute a long time ago, but now it's just annoying. And inappropriate. We are not dating. We are not a couple and seriously, we're more like siblings than anything else, so it's just weird and brings up memories of some TLC shows that I've tried to forget."

Cooper is choking on his root beer and doing a really terrible job of keeping a straight face.

Somehow, I don't think my little talk is making a dent.

"All-righty then," he says. "No more heart references. Good thing Valentine's Day has already passed because I'm not sure how I would describe that shape without sounding like I needed to be censored."

Maybe it's best to just not respond to his comment. He makes me insane. I take a deep breath and rip off a piece of the dark oat bread. "Pass the butter, please."

"You know, they say butter is not very good for the organ that pumps blood throughout your body."

"Cooper."

He laughs.

CHAPTER *Six*

It really doesn't shock me when Cooper shows up that night holding three pizza boxes in his hands.

"Delivery," he says, stepping inside when Mike opens the door.

"Quick, Mike, pay him so he'll go away," I say from the couch.

"I tried that in the sixth grade," Mike says.

"It didn't work," Cooper grins. He sets the pizzas on the counter and the smell of hot marinara sauce and yeasty bread fills the air.

Despite the fact that I was completely stuffed all the way up to the rafters just a few minutes ago from my flat bread and half my cheesecake slice at lunch, I am suddenly salivating.

I don't know what it is about the smell of pizza, but it's seriously almost heavenly.

If I'm going to eat like this every time I come visit Mike, it's probably a good thing this is my first time back in St. Louis. Those puppy scrubs seriously won't fit if I keep coming back here and eating all kinds of carbs and restaurant food.

"Thanks for bringing dinner," Mike says. "Next time, guys, we need to just get a plain spinach salad."

"Yeah. You can get the salad. I really came because I know there's a half slice of leftover s'mores cheesecake in the fridge."

"You touch it, you die," I say, standing from the couch and going in the kitchen with the boys.

Cooper flashes a charming smile at me. "Same old Lyzie."

Mike pulls down paper plates from the cabinet and sets them next to the pizza boxes. "Let's pray." He closes his eyes. "Jesus, please bless this food. Please bless the hands or machinery that prepared it. And please be with Cooper and Eliza and let them be nice to each other. Amen."

I open my eyes and shake my head. "Classy."

"Maybe Jesus can stop the bickering. You guys are like two old cats." Mike picks up a plate and uses it to point at me and Cooper. "Cut it out before I throw both of you out of my apartment."

"Yes sir," Cooper salutes.

I take the plate from Mike. "We're using the fancy plates? What's the occasion?"

"You're home to visit," Mike says, wrapping an arm around my shoulders. "I'm breaking out the good china."

"He means the good Chinet."

Mike snorts.

Sometimes I think it's a little bit of a miracle that I turned out as normal as I am considering that this scene took place basically every single night of my entire existence.

Cooper's mom must not have agreed with the McClowski "never give up" traditions, because she left when Cooper was about five years old. Just packed her bags one day while Cooper was at kindergarten. When she didn't show up to pick him up, his teacher finally called Cooper's dad. Mr. Tom came home with Coop and found a half-empty closet, all of her teapot collection gone and a note that basically said "see you later, but probably not".

I don't think Cooper's really seen his mom since. She came to his high school graduation, I think, but I don't remember much of it. That was the first major event that Dad missed and I was very emotional. I'm pretty sure I blocked it all out of my brain.

So, anyway, Cooper, for at least all the daytime hours, just lived at our house after that. Our house was three houses down the street from him, so Mom would pick up both the boys and me from school, and then Cooper would stay at our house until his dad got home from work. When Mr. Tom worked late, which was often, Cooper would eat dinner with us and do his homework with us. There were a few nights were Cooper just slept on a mat on the opposite wall in Mike's bedroom. He came to church with us every Sunday and I'm pretty sure it was my father who taught Cooper how to throw a baseball, take out the trash and drive.

Basically, he's like the cousin who never went away.

I can tell you the toppings on the pizza before Mike even opens the boxes. This was totally what happened when the boys were in college and I was finishing up high school. Same apartment, same couches, same TV, same paper plates, same pepperoni, three cheese and Hawaiian pizzas.

Every Friday night was pizza night. I think Mike instituted it as a way for us to look forward to the weekend, but it was a good tradition for the three of us that was outside of Mom and Dad and their traditions. Mom was lactose intolerant, so we rarely had pizza around her. Her tradition was Friday night sorbets.

Mom was one of those people who got on the Vitamix train when it first came around and never got off.

It was Mom and the Keva Juice people who kept Vitamix in business, I think.

Those blenders are expensive.

It took me about two years before I could even eat sorbet again without bursting into tears.

"So, I started watching this new TV show," Cooper starts.

"No," Mike and I say in unison.

"Aw, come on, guys. At least let me tell you about it before you decide you don't want to watch it."

"Cooper, you have the absolute *worst* taste in movies ever," I tell him.

"What she said," Mike grins. "I still can't forgive you for *Zoolander*. My eyes have been tainted."

"Says the man who was on the Harrison Ford kick for how many years?"

Mike uses his pizza crust to gesture at Cooper. "Harrison Ford is twice the man you are."

"Gee. Thanks."

"Sorry, man. The jaw line. You've got nothing on him."

Cooper strokes his jaw, speckled with a five o'clock shadow. He got facial hair way before Mike did and never stopped rubbing it in Mike's face for the next two years. "You think? I've been told I have a jaw line only compared to John Wayne."

Mike snorts. "Right. Who told you that?"

"Mrs. Easley."

"Dude, Mrs. Easley told every kid something not true like that. She told me that I looked like I should have been staring in a movie with Doris Day."

I grin. Our high school's ninety-five year old librarian was the nicest old lady in the school. She used to tell me that my hair reminded her of Vivian Leigh's, only it was straight.

My hair looks nothing like Vivian Leigh's. It might be a similar color brown. That's about it.

"Mrs. Easley always told the truth," Cooper insists. "She was always right about my late books."

"I don't think you meant to put an *s* on the end of that word," Mike says.

"Always?"

"Books."

Cooper rolls his eyes and I grin. Cooper's deeply-rooted hate for books is pretty well known. He always claims he's waiting for the movie. Which wasn't super helpful in school.

"So. Two more days of vacation, Lyzie," Cooper says, changing the subject. "What are you guys doing tomorrow?"

I shrug and look at Mike who shrugs and looks at me. "I don't know," I say, finally. "I'm sure we will think of something. I'm going back in the morning the day after tomorrow, though. I need to do a few things and go to the grocery store and get in bed at a good time before my shift on Monday. Plus, I'd kind of like to make church, if I can."

Katie started us going to the late service at church, likely so she can sit with Luke. So, every Sunday I'm off, I get to sleep in until ten and it's amazing.

And it's awesome, because even though I'm going to be leaving here in time for church, I still won't have to leave until like eight.

Katie and Ashten call eight o'clock halfway through the day.

They are just odd. But it's a very good thing that the two of them are so compatible with their early rising times and that they live all the way across the street where I don't have to hear them first thing in the morning.

"Better make tomorrow count then," Cooper says. "I guess we should probably go bowling."

"And probably not."

"Ah, come on, Lyzie. You love to bowl."

"I do not love to bowl and you know it." I eat my Hawaiian pizza and watch Mike turn on the TV to Netflix. "Let's go to the zoo."

Mike snorts. "Why?"

"Why do you ever go to the zoo?" I wave my pizza slice at him. "To go look at the animals. Duh."

"Such a nineties expression," Mike says to me. "No, I meant, why do you want to go to zoo? Have we ever even been to the zoo?"

"I went on a field trip one time," I say. "I think I was in the third grade."

"Yep," Cooper nods. "Mrs. Beckingham's class always went to the zoo. I think it was her way of coping with the last couple of weeks of chaos before summer hit."

"I mean, I guess we can go to the zoo," Mike says all slowly, chewing his pizza. "Is it kind of weird for a group of adults to go to the zoo? Do you need a kid to get in or something?"

"This is just a guess, but I'm assuming the zoo would prefer that we come alone as opposed to kidnapping a child," Cooper says.

"Surely we know a little kid we could take with us."

We all sit there for a few minutes, quietly chewing as we think.

"Nope," Cooper declares.

"Me either," Mike says. "You work with kids, Lyzie. Can we borrow one of them?"

"I work with *newborns*, Mike. And I'm pretty certain that none of their mothers would let me take them to the zoo. And if they did, I might have to turn them into the child protection people."

"Let's go just us. It would be way easier to not have to stop and blow boogery noses or use the bathroom every ten minutes anyway," Cooper says.

"You don't know too much about children, do you?" I ask Cooper.

"I didn't babysit too much, no."

"Smart parents."

Saturday morning and we're at the St. Louis Zoo with the rest of the city.

Apparently, a beautiful Saturday morning at the zoo appealed to a lot of other people too. And a lot of them don't even have children with them. Most of them do. But a good amount don't.

Proof that I am, in fact, relatively normal.

I don't remember inviting him, but Cooper is here anyway. He is wearing a safari hat and khaki shorts because he's Cooper and he's weird. Mike is squinting at the monkeys behind his sunglasses and reading every single plaque we pass because he's Mike and he thinks too much, even at the zoo.

I'm on the lookout for ice cream or a Frappucino or something icy. It's only ten o'clock, but it's already getting warm. Besides, when you think about it, ice cream is probably healthier than most breakfast cereals.

I'm looking at you, Froot Loops.

"Wow, listen to this," Mike says for the twenty-third time and we've only been at the zoo for an hour.

"No," Cooper says to him.

"No, really, this is super interesting about the differences between monkeys and apes!"

"We don't care," I tell Mike.

"We want to see the polar bears."

"No, we want ice cream."

"We want to share our ice cream with a penguin."

"No, we don't. Penguins carry disease."

"Uh, only if the disease is called *cuteness*."

I shake my head at Cooper. "Why are you here?"

He slings an arm around my shoulders and pulls me into his side. "Because deep down, you know that you would be completely bored to tears without me."

"Mm-hmm."

"You love me, Eliza Wakeman. And one of these days, you're going to admit it."

I just sigh. "Cooper. The odds of that are probably about as good as an ape growing a tail."

"That's what I was going to tell you guys about!" Mike says. "Apes don't have tails! It's how you can tell the species apart."

Cooper just grins.

CHAPTER *Seven*

"How was your trip, Eliza?" Ashten passes me the basket full of homemade rolls and smiles next to me at Katie's dining table.

It's six-thirty on Tuesday night and I'm finally able to catch up with Katie and Ashten. And in a surprise twist, there was a mystery guest invited to dinner tonight. He showed up late, but he did show up.

Luke is sitting next to Katie and my friend is looking beautiful in a black sleeveless top and faded skinny jeans. Despite the casualness of the outfit, I know she changed specifically for this dinner. I'm fairly certain that the reason Katie works from home is so she can stay in her pajamas all day. There have been multiple times when I've shown up for an impromptu dinner and she's wearing plaid jammy bottoms, slippers and a sweatshirt jacket that is about one step removed from a robe. It's sort of on the same plain as those crocheted or knit duster things everyone was wearing a few years ago where you could never be sure if they meant to wear their jammies out in public or not.

"The trip was good," I say, taking a roll and breathing in the scent. "Dear gracious, Katie, did you make these rolls?"

"Maybe," Katie grins.

I hold the incredibly soft, yeasty roll so it's almost touching my nose. "Are they the cloverleaf rolls just shaped differently?"

She is still smirking. "Maybe."

"I love you."

"I know," she says, pulling a Han Solo and passing me the butter. "I doubled the batch, so eat up."

"You really hate my puppy pants, don't you?"

Katie and Ashten both laugh.

Luke is too busy having a moment with his own roll to question my comment. His eyes are closed, his hand not holding the roll is raised. I think he's about to burst into some sort of chorus.

Not necessarily a bad thing. Luke is a great singer. He's apparently in pretty high demand around these parts for weddings and the like. I looked him up after Katie introduced us for the first time just to make sure my friend wasn't interested some weirdo and found his prices for weddings on his site. Considering that he's been booked every weekend for months, let's just say that he's likely living on the more comfortable side of the equation.

If only I could sing. Maybe there's a market for singers who can't necessarily hit all the right notes but they at least sing with enthusiasm.

"Luke?" Katie asks, elbowing him lightly in the ribs.

"Shh," Luke hushes her in a whisper. "You are interrupting them."

"Interrupting who?"

"Whom. Ridiculous that I have to correct an editor on her English."

Ashten snorts.

"Interrupting *whom*?" Katie asks, rolling her eyes.

"The roll angels. Shh."

"You're weird."

He holds his hand higher. "Shh! Listen!" he commands.

We all freeze and a couple of seconds later, Luke starts humming and then singing, first quietly and then at the top of his lungs. "'Glory, glory, hallelujah!'"

"Oh, good grief," Katie says, waving her hand in dismissal. "You guys are ridiculous. It's like you've never had a roll before."

"Darling, it's like I've been eating gluten-free my whole life until this very moment," Luke says. "And let me just tell you, I have had some pretty amazing breads before, so this means a lot."

Ashten and I very politely pretend not to notice the fact that Luke just called Katie "darling". And we also pretend not to notice that her cheeks suddenly pink up like she was just cast in a Maybelline ad.

But we might exchange a look of joy that lasts .003 seconds.

Katie has wanted this for so long. I'm so excited for her. And I make a mental note to pray even more tirelessly for her and this new potential relationship.

Luke is a good guy, from everything I've seen about him. He needs to be if he's going to deserve Katie.

"So, what all did you do in St. Louis?" Ashten asks, changing the conversation back to my trip. It's unfortunate, because everything in me wants to immediately begin dicing through the potential of Luke and Katie here. Is he serious about her? Is she serious about him? Are they both serious about Jesus? Who is going to be the primary breadwinner and who is going to stay home with the children? Oh my goodness, do they even want children? Does he even *like* children?

I eat my roll to stop my mental hyperventilating.

Men ruin everything. If he weren't here, I could be verbally dumping this stuff out of my brain and moving on. Since I've had to stuff it back in though, I'll probably end up with a migraine from all the pressure of it building up inside.

Though, I guess if he weren't here, I wouldn't be having these thoughts in the first place.

And that, my friends, is what you call a double-edged sword.

Ashten and Katie are just looking at me expectantly and I realize that I was asked a question that I never answered. Luke is still too busy humming over his roll to be expecting an answer.

"Sorry, what did you ask?" I say.

"What did you do on your trip?" Ashten asks louder, like maybe I didn't answer because I have suddenly gone deaf.

Can you even suddenly go deaf? I mean, I guess that girl suddenly went blind in that horse jumping movie, *Wild Hearts Can't Be Broken*, or something like that. She was just going about her normal day, brushing her hair and whatever and *boom*. Blind.

Or was that Mary from *Little House on the Prairie*?

I don't remember now.

"Um," I say, trying to get my brain to focus on her question. This is what happens when I don't get an iced coffee in the afternoon. My brain just sort of goes to the functionality of dry rot. I can still absorb stuff but nothing good is coming out.

I need to go to bed.

"The. Trip," Ashten says, snapping in my face and annunciating every syllable. "Good night, Eliza. You're worse than my kinder guys tonight. Are you okay?"

I rub my cheek. "Sorry. Too much going on and not enough caffeine to compensate." I didn't even have work today and I'm still this scatterbrained. I'm working the next three days.

It might get interesting.

Hopefully the hospital doesn't have a lawsuit coming it's way this week on account of me. You don't work as a postnatal nurse for

87

very long before hearing THE STORY about the tired, running around like crazy nurse who accidentally swapped babies between patients and now the hospital is out three million dollars and the nurse is working as a greeter at Walmart.

Though, I partially blame the hospital for my dependence on caffeine. The cafeteria has an espresso machine in it. It's four dollars for the first cup and fifty cents for refills. There's usually a line, especially at the seven o'clock hours when the shift changes over. One day, the machine went out and almost every employee at the hospital was basically comatose.

"The trip was fine," I tell Ashten. "We didn't do very much. Ate pizza. Went to the zoo."

Ashten grins. "The zoo?"

"Why is everyone all freaked out about us going to the zoo? Other people go to the zoo all the time."

Katie shrugs. "I don't know anyone who has been to the zoo since elementary school."

"Well, I mean, I go at least once a year but I'm also a teacher," Ashten says. "The St. Louis Zoo is fantastic but the bus ride to get there last about forty-seven years."

"I can imagine," I tell her.

Luke grins at me. "Did you at least enjoy the zoo?"

"We did. It was hot but it was fun." I'm trying my best to not mention that Cooper hung out with us the entire weekend.

Katie and Ashten would totally jump all over that one. I've mentioned him in the past to both of them and they both had like a million questions about him and his constant proposals. He's officially a taboo topic when it comes to the two of them. Nothing I say appeases them. It's like neither of them can understand why I am not falling all over myself to say yes to the Cooper package and why I would rather have adventure and excitement instead of complacency and boring-ness.

Sometimes I feel like Belle from *Beauty and the Beast* and they are the not-so-understanding townspeople. I'm standing at the edge of the town square singing "I WANT ADVENTURE" at the top of my lungs and they are shaking their heads and passing me rolls from their little carts.

I mean, the roll part is good. The being misunderstood part is not. I don't even necessarily want to find a Beast, I just want to see and experience things beyond my everyday existence and the Gaston guy I grew up with.

Though Cooper is way nicer than Gaston. And not nearly as conceited.

I need to stop with this comparison before I hurt my head more.

"So, Luke, do you have another wedding this weekend?" I ask, moving the conversation off of me and my trip before Cooper comes up or I start bursting into *Beauty and the Beast* songs. Ashten is still looking at me but Katie turns her attention to Luke.

I have a feeling I'll get pulled aside by Ashten before I leave tonight.

She doesn't leave well enough alone.

"Yep," Luke says to me. "I'm pretty much booked through September."

It's only the third week in March. "Holy cow," I say.

"It's wedding season. March to October-ish are just insane."

"Luke, that's way more than a season. That's like three seasons," I tell him.

"I guess you're right. Anyway, the winter is my slow season. But I've been booked through the summer since last July."

"That's insane."

"You're telling me." Luke rubs the back of his neck. "I have been threatening to go on a silent trip by myself at the end of September. Just me somewhere in a little cabin in the woods by myself so I don't have to use my vocal cords and they can have a vacation."

I don't know Luke very well but based on what I do know, I can't see a trip like that going super well for him. He's too social. You can tell he doesn't do the introverted thing very well.

I have done a lot of thinking on this and I'm pretty sure I'm one of those closet introverts. Most people would probably say I'm extroverted, but really, deep down, I actually like being alone.

It's part of why I've enjoyed living by myself so much. I work all day surrounded by people and being needed and calming patients and doctors and other nurses down. It's nice to go home to my house and sit by myself. I've thought about getting a dog but then I'd just have something else that needs me at home.

So, no dog. I tried the plant thing last fall. It did not go well.

Charlie Brown had better luck caring for a Christmas tree than I did growing some bulbs that were supposedly idiot-proof according to the lady at Lowe's.

I feel like she basically just backhandedly offended me.

"What's your favorite song that you sing?" I ask Luke.

Luke has a very similar style to Michael Buble. Lots of oldies, lots of classy lyrics, lots of big band music. It's pretty much awesome.

Luke shrugs. "I don't know. It varies. It usually depends on my mood and the mood of the audience. Some crowds handle the quicker tempos better than others. I tend to feed off the vibe in the room."

I could see that.

"Ever written a song?" Ashten asks.

"Once," Luke nods. "I tried it out at a wedding. No one danced. No one clapped. Not one person even got teary-eyed. So, I decided to leave the song writing to those with more talent."

"Well, what was the song about?" Ashten asks.

"I was trying to pay homage to one of my favorite childhood movies," Luke says.

"Which is what?" she persists.

"*Rookie of the Year.*"

All of us immediately start groaning.

"Dude," I say, shaking my head.

"Really? That's really the movie that inspired a song?" Ashten asks.

"I mean, it's about a kid who broke his arm and then plays baseball," Katie says. "You honestly sang that at a wedding?"

Luke sighs. "I should have figured none of you people would understand. Where is another man when I need one? I'll have you know that *Rookie of the Year* is one of the most inspiring, emotional movies I have ever seen."

"Luke, I really mean this in the nicest way possible, but you really need to expand your pathetic taste in movies," I say.

"That wasn't really very nice," Luke says.

"We can start tonight," Ashten nods. "We need to get you into deeper movie waters, my friend."

"Actually, I have plans tonight..."

"What do we think would be best?" Katie asks, ignoring Luke. "Nicholas Sparks? Or would that be like making him jump off the side and into the deep end? Do we need to slowly introduce him to the adult pool? I mean, *Rookie of the Year* is basically the kiddie sprinklers in the yard. I don't think it even technically counts as a pool."

"Maybe we need to do a floaty movie tonight," Ashten nods. "A shallow end with floaties movie."

They are totally about to lose me on the analogy here. But the look on Luke's face, I'm not the only one.

"Oh! I've got it! *Walk to Remember!*" Katie shouts.

"No, no! *Hope Floats!*" Ashten says. Apparently, she is taking the floaty thing literally.

"Guys!" I say, putting my hands on my temples and closing my eyes. "You don't read *Boxcar Children* and then go straight to *Sherlock Holmes*. And you don't watch *Mr. Rogers' Neighborhood* and then move straight over to *The Sixth Sense*. You both are getting too advanced here. He likes kids' movies. Rather than go straight to adult fare, start with the preteen stuff. *Princess Diaries*. Something like that."

"*Princess Diaries!*" they both shout together.

"Oh boy," Luke says, shaking his head. He looks at me. "Come on, Eliza. I thought you were helping me there for a little bit."

"And done," Ashten nods, clearing our dishes. "Katie, Eliza and I will clean up. You and Luke go get the movie ready." She marches to the sink with our dishes and I pick up the bread basket, my job assigned.

Luke and Katie disappear into the family room and Ashten sidelines me by the sink.

"You saw him, didn't you?" she asks, half blocking me in so I can't get away.

"Luke? Of course I saw him. I was sitting right next to him."

"Not Luke." Ashten rolls her eyes. "You know exactly who I mean."

My sigh sounds more like a growl.

"See? I knew you saw him." She grins. "Tell me about him."

"No."

"Please?"

"No."

"I promise I won't tell Katie."

I might have smiled.

CHAPTER *Eight*

Three mamas and four babies today. My cup officially runneth over. I'm running down the hallway, my badge lanyard flipping over my shoulder as I go. I've got one brand new mom in major pain from her c-section and a mother of twins who is requesting some breastfeeding assistance, while my other mom is having some fairly large clots that are making me a little concerned.

I page my bleeding mother's doctor, I pull a narcotic for my c-section mama, administer it into her IV and head in to assist my multiples mother.

And people say we all sit up here in rocking chairs and knit on the fifth floor.

Right.

We are booked up today. I don't know what is nine months before mid-March, but apparently it was a loving time for a lot of people.

Too much information.

Sarah is the twins' mother and the boy and girl are her first babies. I haven't heard her whole story yet. She delivered yesterday and has been pretty tired today, so I've tried to stay out of the room unless I'm doing my blood pressure and fundal checks so she and her husband can rest.

I go in and the husband is gone but a woman who is obviously Sarah's mother is there, sitting on the other bed in the room with a baby in her arms. Sarah has the other baby in the rocking chair.

"Hi there," I say, bright and cheerfully. "How is everyone in here?" I wash up to my elbows in scalding hot water and get three paper towels to dry off.

Sarah's eyes are red, whether from exhaustion or tears, I'm not sure. A TV is showing something on HGTV but the sound isn't on.

"She's not eating," she says to me and I hear the catch in her throat.

Tears are definitely the cause of the redness.

Poor girl.

I grab a few pillows off the bed and adjust them around Sarah, picking up the baby and moving Sarah's arms around. "Let's try a different position," I say. The baby girl is wide awake. Her brother is completely sacked out on his grandma and based on the look of just sheer joy on the older woman's face, I'm willing to bet that these are the first grandbabies of this household.

I finish adjusting the pillows and then set the baby so her feet slip behind her mom and her face is directly in front of Sarah's chest.

"Okay, so this is called the football hold," I say and I do my best to talk Sarah through everything I'm doing so it removes some of the awkwardness of it. Sarah is more desperate than modest at this point, so she does everything I say without even flinching. The baby girl kind of half-noses her mother and then closes her eyes and is immediately asleep.

You know that saying "sleep like a baby"? I think this is where it comes from. I've seen newborns fall asleep faster than Cooper can inhale an espresso.

You think I'm addicted to caffeine, you've never met Cooper. There's a reason he's so chipper.

"Oh no," Sarah moans. "She did it again!"

Sarah's mother chuckles lightly from the bed. "Back asleep?"

"It's like the second she gets close to me she passes out!" Sarah's exclamation is more shrill than sarcastic and I hear the worry behind it.

"That's a good sign. It means she already knows who her mama is and she's comfortable with you," I tell her, keeping my voice a soothing, low tone to try and calm Sarah's heart rate down. I check my notes on Sarah's delivery and see she had Demerol during her labor.

I glance up at the white board on the wall to jog my memory on the babies' names. "So Zachary has been nursing okay, right?" I ask her, picking up the baby girl again.

"Zach has been nursing like a champ. He wakes up, eats and goes right back to sleep. But Ainsley just doesn't want to eat at all."

I set the baby girl in the plastic bassinet and check her birth weight on my chart. She was about ten ounces lighter than her brother, maybe the Demerol affected her a little more than it did him.

I feel like half of nursing is just trying to figure out answers. The other half of nursing is trying to figure out the question so you can find out the answer.

"Okay," I say, clicking off my electronic chart and slipping it back into my pocket. "She's probably still pretty tired from the labor and delivery. And right now, your body is still producing colostrum, so while it's not essential that she is nursing, it's still really good for her and it's going to help get your milk in faster. So let's try something else." I stick the "Do Not Disturb" sign on the door just in case any visitors decide to pop by and turn back to Sarah.

"How comfortable are you with your mom being here while we try a few different things?" I ask her in a low voice.

Sarah waves her hand. "Oh my gosh, I don't care. Mom was there for the whole delivery yesterday. And the whole labor the day before. Gosh, she was even there when we technically got pregnant. She's already seen everything."

I guess my face registers the shock that I'm trying my best to conceal because Sarah's mom immediately starts laughing. "Sarah, you have *got* to stop telling people that!" she says.

Sarah grins at me and the lines of frustration and exhaustion are temporarily smoothed on her face. I begin unswaddling little Ainsley and unsnapping her little onesie shirt.

"We got pregnant with the twins through IVF," Sarah tells me. "Danny was obviously there for the egg retrieval and all that, but he had to go out of town on an emergency business trip for the embryo transfer day, so Mom came with me so I wouldn't have to be there by myself." She smiles at her babies. "Though, I guess I wasn't technically alone since these guys were there too."

The look that passes over her face as she looks at her babies is one that I only see on a handful of women through here. I have no doubt that the vast majority of moms I see love their babies but there's just something different about the way the moms look at their babies when they have also struggled with infertility.

If I hadn't done postpartum nursing, I had seriously considered working as a nurse in a fertility clinic.

I smile at Sarah. "You are a very brave and wonderful mom."

Though she was grinning two seconds ago, she immediately dissolves into tears. I've got Ainsley naked except for her diaper and I carry her over to Sarah, lightly squeezing Sarah's shoulder.

"All right, Mom," I say to her. "This is where it gets fun. Sometimes babies eat better if they are skin to skin, so let's see if that wakes her up a bit."

I go soak a clean washcloth in ice cold water, wring it out and carry it over to Sarah and baby Ainsley. Sarah has unrobed the top half of her and she's got Ainsley all snuggled up against her.

I always feel like a bad guy doing this to some poor, innocent newborn baby, but the end result is worth it.

I get Ainsley situated back in the football hold and then reach behind Sarah and set the ice cold washcloth on Ainsley's feet.

She immediately jumps and starts wimpering and then latches herself right on to Sarah.

"It worked!" Sarah is crying too and I watch for a couple of minutes to make sure her latch looks good before I decide to let the two of them cry together.

"Okay, I'll check back on you guys in a bit. I've got the 'Do Not Disturb' sign on the door, so feel free to just sit like this with her as long as you need to. No one will be coming in. Have the birth certificate people been by yet?"

Sarah nods. "They came this morning."

"Great. So I'll be back in just a while. Pain level okay?"

She nods, caressing her baby's head and I smile.

"You're doing great, mama. Keep it up."

I leave and make a few notes in the chart. Since the whole breastfeeding initiative that this hospital has adopted, we now have to keep some pretty serious records of every time we watch a baby feed before we can discharge them. It's a good thing because it helps with breastfeeding success but it makes my day that much longer.

I have a quick break, so I run downstairs to the espresso machine. Predictably, there's a line all the way to the cash register.

"Good grief," I say, standing behind another nurse in teal scrubs.

Sometimes you can tell what floor a nurse is from by her scrubs. The children's hospital nurses always wear cartoon characters all over themselves. The ER nurses are always no nonsense in teal. There's a school in town that uses our hospital for clinicals, since we're a teaching hospital, and they always show up as this sea of royal purple.

A lot of times, I meet people in this line and we chat small talk for a few minutes while we wait. But, this lady ahead of me is texting or Facebooking on her phone and obviously is trying to just mentally check out for a few minutes.

I get it, but at the same time, I feel like technology has totally separated us from each other.

I finally get to the front of the line about five minutes later and get myself a caramel latte. The machine is not fancy but it's also cheap.

101

Cheap and caffeinated, two of my favorite words. I pay the cashier and drink as much as I can on the elevator ride back up to the fifth floor.

It always takes a few hours for my adrenaline to settle down after I get off work. Either that, or maybe it just takes a few hours for the caffeine high to finally wear off. Either way, I'm still pretty wired when I get off at seven, so I decide I should maybe go work out. As a part of our work benefits, we get access to this gym across the street from the hospital. It's a great gym and it's gigantic, but since it's so close and it's all hospital staff who work out there, I feel like I haven't really left work when I go, so I'm rarely there.

Still, it's a good gym. I dig a pair of yoga pants out of the trunk of my car, change in the locker room and go run on the treadmill while Rachael Ray cooks up something incredibly unhealthy in thirty minutes on the TV in front of me.

There's something cathartic to working out while someone is frying something in butter in front of you. I'm not sure what it is. It is probably the Pharisee coming out in me.

"Excuse me, is this machine taken?"

It's a younger guy with no shirt standing next to the treadmill beside me as I start my cool down walk. He's smiling all coy at me.

Okay, people. Note to all men out there: This is not a good way to ask a girl out.

First, I'm gross and I do not like attention when I feel gross. Second, I'm obviously here after work which means I just need some time to wind down by myself. Third, put a shirt on. Fourth, the treadmill is obviously not taken because duh, there is no one on it. So rather than be dumb, just get on the treadmill, do your run and find somewhere else to pick up girls.

I almost share my mental speech with the guy but I don't want to get into it, so I just say, "It looks like it's free," and go back to watching Rachael, hoping he'll take the hint.

He doesn't.

"So, I'm Sam," he says.

I don't respond.

He's persistent, this one. He's still talking. He's taking after his namesake, which I can only assume was that annoying little guy who kept pestering the bigger guy to eat the green eggs and ham. He says, "I'm hoping you're like this treadmill after you're done here."

Now I look sharply at him, frowning. "Excuse me?"

"Free? I hope you're free after this?" He winces and rubs the back of his neck. "Sorry, that uh, kind of...sounded better in my head."

I can't help it. I start laughing.

He grins, still rubbing the back of his neck. "So, the laughing. Is that a good sign that you'll go out with me after this?"

I smash the red button on my treadmill and hop off. "Nope, sorry. I don't go out with strangers."

"Well. I'm Sam," he says again. "And you're...?"

"Not going out tonight. Besides, you're just starting your workout and I'm just finishing mine." I grab my water bottle and keys and start walking for the door.

"Maybe next time!" he calls out after me. Thankfully he doesn't follow me or I would have to go all *Miss Congenialty*'s S-I-N-G self-defense moves on him. Mike has made me too paranoid about things. He's likely just a lonely man hoping for a bite to eat alongside some conversation.

Thanks to my dear older brother, though, I immediately am concerned about a kidnapper. Mike was forever telling me about how Ted Bundy, the infamous serial killer, was supposedly this super good looking man who didn't look the least bit like the violent murderer he actually was.

"You can't be too careful, Lyzie," Mike was always saying. He would make me call him whenever I was leaving for someplace and whenever I got there, all through high school.

Maybe Mike went a little overboard, but when I think about the burden he carried for me after Dad died and especially after Mom got sick, I just start feeling bad that I argued so much with Mike over his little rules.

They've obviously kept me safe so far.

I get to my car, lock my doors and call my brother as I drive home, clicking the call to my car's bluetooth.

"Well, if it isn't the Prodigal who left and came home and left again."

Cooper's voice booms into my car and I immediately break the traffic laws and look at my phone while I'm driving.

"Didn't I call Mike?"

"Mike's otherwise engaged so he told me to answer it. Mike's phone, this is Cooper."

"What's Mike doing?"

"I don't know. He's making something for dinner because I'm starving and I've been working all day. He's a good wifey."

"I'm so glad you have each other," I say, rolling my eyes.

I can almost hear Cooper's grin. "So, how was your day?" he asks me.

"Fine. I worked and then went to the gym. Some guy was trying to talk to me by the treadmills."

"I hope you didn't try to run away from him because you wouldn't be going anywhere, even if you were running very fast."

There's a reason I don't call and talk to Cooper often, despite the emails he always sends me.

"Is Mike done cooking yet?"

"No, now he's scrambling eggs."

"What is he making?"

"I think he said something about chicken fried rice."

Mike can only make about five different dishes, but the ones he does make are really good. When we were kids, Dad's favorite place to eat was a teppan grill here in town. I remember Mike being in junior-high and coming home and trying to replicate the fried rice.

He's really good at it now. But he should be. He's had twenty years of experience.

My mouth is watering. Especially since I have officially worked out through an appropriate time for inviting myself over to Katie and Ashten's for dinner. Those two are probably already in bed.

Apparently, I come by my late dinner time naturally.

"So the guy who was talking to you, was he kind of shrimpy and ugly looking? Like that little red dude in the mermaid movie?"

"What?" I ask. I can hear Mike demanding to know what guy Cooper is talking about in the background.

"You know. The red-haired mermaid with the little lobster friend?"

"I mean, he was human."

"Always a good first step. One that the guy who fell in love with the mermaid should have adhered to."

"Seriously, you are the hardest person on the planet to talk to."

"Now, you can't say that. Have you talked to everyone else on the planet? Based on your fear of flying, I would doubt it."

"I am not scared of flying."

"The last time you flew, you threw up all over the poor lady in front of you and spent the rest of the flight in the bathroom."

"That's because I was embarrassed, not because I'm scared of flying," I tell him.

My heart hurts for my poor eleven year-old self. I had braces and stringy, greasy hair and I couldn't sing worth a flip and yet somehow I was on my very first plane ride ever flying to California for a singing competition with the girls' chorus from my school.

It just had all the makings of one of those 80's coming of age movies.

And I will forever regret the day that Cooper and Mike found out about all of it.

I haven't flown since. The closest I've been to flying has been picking up Katie from the airport. The fact that she flies across the country every three weeks, sometimes more often, is just completely bizarre to me.

I mean, my stomach is cringing just thinking about it. It doesn't mesh well with my desire to have adventures in other parts of this country and other ones, but I'm still working on that.

Anyway.

"Is Mike done yet?" I ask.

"Nope. Adding in the chicken and rice now. Dear goodness, it smells amazing over here. I wish you had smell-o-phone. Though considering what this apartment usually smells like, it's probably good you don't."

Again, I hear Mike protesting in the background and Cooper laughs.

"Okay, well, can you just have him call me when he's done entertaining the riffraff off the streets?" I ask.

"You should be so lucky to talk to this kind of entertaining riffraff. I bet the guy at the gym wasn't nearly as much fun to talk to. What did he do? Ask you which way the beach was?"

"No, but that probably would have been a better pick up line than the one he came up with. Especially considering he was shirtless."

"Shirtless? Now that's just poor taste. I mean, trying to get a date in a gym is poor taste to begin with but shirtless is just a new level of low. I mean, if it were me, which it wouldn't have been because I wouldn't be shirtless in a gym in the first place, if it were me

108

trying to get a date with you, I would have just come right out and asked."

"Oh, this I know."

"I would have said something like, 'Hey, pretty lady, would you like to have dinner with me?' And you would have been like, 'You obviously are an attractive guy who works out and loves Jesus. Sure, I'll go out with you.'"

I have to laugh. "Oh Cooper."

"Did that work? Because, hey, pretty lady—"

"Cooper!" I yell.

"Fine, fine. Well, Eliza, it was great talking with you, but it smells like the Chinatown part of heaven in here, so I'm going to have to sign out."

"You are such a product of the digital age. You don't sign out of a phone call."

"Peace out?"

"Good-bye, Cooper."

"Bye, Lyzie."

The line clicks and I look at the phone. Cooper has hung up.

Looks like I won't be talking to Mike.

I roll my eyes and pull into my garage, closing the door behind me and going into the empty house.

Maybe I should revisit the idea of a dog.

I remind myself of the eating and going for walks and things getting chewed and the pooper-scooper-ing and shake my head.

Or not.

But still. Sometimes I can seriously creep myself out living alone.

I make myself a peanut butter and jelly sandwich, wash it down with a cup of decaf and head toward the bed.

CHAPTER *Nine*

"Glad everyone could make it here tonight." Katie is sitting down with her Bible on the one open spot on their fireplace hearth on Wednesday night. Her house is packed. People are all over the couches, all over the floor and there's a good crowd gathered in the kitchen.

It's ridiculous. We have got to move this study somewhere else.

Like I said, though, the appeal is that it's at a house and not a church. Maybe we can rent out a coffeehouse or something.

"If you're new here," Katie starts the same speech she says every week. "If you're new here, we kind of facilitate the discussion, but really, we want everyone to participate. So every week, we'll tell you what section of the chapter we're reading next and then when you come back, you can have it read and we'll talk through it. So this week, we were all reading in James chapter one. So, um, Luke? Can you read the first four verses for us, please?"

Luke nods and starts reading. "'James, a bond-servant of God and of the Lord Jesus Christ, to the twelve tribes who are dispersed abroad: Greetings. Consider it all joy, my brethren, when you encounter various trials, knowing that the testing of your faith produces endurance. And let endurance have its perfect result, so that you may be perfect and complete, lacking in nothing.'"

Katie looks up from her Bible. "All-righty, let's open the floor up. What did you guys see in this chapter this week?"

I can already tell you who is going to talk first. His name is David, he's a single guy in his mid-thirties and he thinks he knows everything about the Bible because he went to seminary and he has a beard.

Apparently, seminary and a beard makes you the World's Most Primary Scholar On All Things Biblical And/Or Sociological In Nature.

Plus, he wears glasses. Plastic-framed black ones.

He knows All.

Poor guy. I probably need to give him grace. I don't really even know him. I try my best to avoid his corner of the room when we are doing the visit and snack after the study is over. He's usually talking with a bunch of people about social injustices or the floundering legal system or the perils of our government and the leaders in it. Not exactly lighthearted, Hump Day conversation.

So, I usually just do my thing in the kitchen. Sometimes, I talk to people. Sometimes, I make coffee. Sometimes, I just give up on being social and go home.

Sometimes, Ashten comes with me and Katie calls us both from her bedroom and yells at us to get back over to her house because this Bible study was mostly our idea.

Which is kind of funny, I'm not going to lie.

Katie is cute when she's mad.

Just as I predicted, despite the couple of other people who raised their hands like they are in the second grade, David just starts talking. "Well, coming from an ecclesiastical perspective, I just don't think we can jump right into this book without at least briefly discoursing about the life of James and the apostolic church," he says.

I'm immediately making a mental note to start a page on Petition.org to strike the word *discourse* from the English language.

It just sounds bad.

Katie, as the discussion facilitator, nods politely even though I know she's inwardly cringing. "Okay, that's a fair point," she says. "Did anyone do any research on James and his background?"

Luke jumps in before David can answer and tie us up for the next twenty minutes doing a monologue. "He was an apostle, he was a leader in the church, he could have potentially been Jesus' brother and he was writing to a church that was under pretty severe persecution."

Katie nods. "Great. Okay. Anyone have any thoughts on the first verse?"

One of the girls who has been coming for a few weeks, I can't remember her name, starts talking. "I found it interesting that even though the church is dispersed and likely all experiencing different things in the places they were dispersed to, that James still just wrote one letter to all of them. He knew it would be applicable for all believers, no matter what circumstances they were in."

"Great point," Katie says.

"So I started looking up the word 'bondservant' this week," Ashten says.

I smile. Ashten is our word girl. One night, she made a poster board showing all the different meanings of the word *love* and all the different Greek and Hebrew words that translate to it. She's totally a teacher down to the core.

"It was really interesting," she continues. "I think the meaning that I took to heart the most was one I saw that said something along the lines of a servant who is devoted to someone else without regard for their own interests. So, that's basically what we are called to be. Devoted to Jesus and devoted to each other and not focused on our own selves or our own interests."

Everyone around the room is nodding, which is pretty typical response for Ashten. She's one of those girls that I wish I could be more like.

The discussion continues and I'm stuck to the words "lacking in nothing" that James says in verse four.

"So that you may be perfect and complete, lacking in nothing."

I don't feel like I'm lacking in anything.

Am I lacking in something?

I can clearly see where my friends feel like they are lacking. Katie wants to be married with all her heart, so I know she feels like she's lacking in the husband department. I'm just praying hard that Luke is the one and if he's not, I'm praying that she finds out quickly so she isn't wasting her time.

Ashten likely feels the same way about a husband. I guess I don't know. I've never asked her what her hopes for marriage are. I know she was dating someone seriously before we met and it ended pretty badly. But I know she feels like she's lacking in the family department. Her relationship with her brother has been kind of estranged lately.

And then there's me.

I mean, I'm not married. But I don't really feel like I'm lacking anything. I have a great job, I have great friends and I get along with my brother, especially now that he lives a good hour and a half from me.

Distance makes the heart grow fonder.

"Well, I think that's pretty good for tonight," Katie says, looking at her watch. "I think Sabrina, Anna and Kevin brought some snacks, so feel free to hang out for a couple of minutes."

Most people would hear this and interpret it to mean "stay as long as you want". Katie literally means "a couple of minutes". Come nine o'clock, everyone had better be gone or mean Katie comes out.

She doesn't mess around when it comes time to put her pajama pants on.

I have actually heard her tell someone who had the audacity to linger that she wished she was at their house so she could leave and go home.

They didn't get the very unsubtle hint.

It was probably David.

Bad Eliza.

I find myself in the kitchen with a few girls and we talk small talk until everyone leaves at nine. It doesn't take too many weeks of being growled at by your hostess before you learn the right time to leave.

By nine o'clock, everyone except me, Luke, Ashten and Katie are out of the house. Katie closes the door behind the last straggler and sighs, looking at her living room.

"I mean, it's like we let a herd of elephants through here," she grouses, straightening pillows and picking up Styrofoam cups. "Did these people not have mothers? Do they not know about trash cans?"

Luke grins at me and Ashten and pulls out the vacuum.

Katie says basically the same speech every single Wednesday night at nine o'clock. She's a creature of habit, that one.

Luke vacuums, Ashten and I clean the kitchen, Katie puts all the chairs and pillows back where they go and by nine-fifteen, the house is back to looking like the page out of the Pottery Barn catalog like it typically looks. My style is a little more farmhouse, Katie's is totally traditional and beautiful.

I head home a few minutes later. I'm working in the morning and there's this thought in the back of my head like maybe if I actually go to bed when I'm supposed to, I won't have to rely on that espresso machine at the hospital tomorrow.

The odds are not good, but you never know.

It didn't work. Four o'clock and here I am, standing in line behind two pediatric doctors, who sound like are completing their residency here, based on my subtle eavesdropping. I fill up my cup with a mocha this time and drink it as fast as I can as I go back to the elevator.

I climb into the almost full elevator car and ask the man standing by the door to push the fifth floor button for me. It's so full that we stop every floor and every time we dump people off, more people get back on.

I don't mind. It gives me more time to drink my coffee without scalding my tongue.

"Well, hi there, elusive treadmill lady."

I look up after we stop on the third floor and it's the shirtless Sam, though now he's wearing not just a button down shirt but also a doctor's coat.

He really needs to work on his pickup line game. I mean, the man is a decent-looking *doctor*, for goodness' sake. Surely he could just start with that instead of all of these cheesy lines. Something like, "Hi. I'm a doctor."

It's not too hard.

I look at his nametag. *Dr. Samuel Wilmington.*

Very Ivy League sounding name.

"Hi," I say to him as he steps onto the elevator. He scoots around a couple of people and stands next to me, nodding to my Styrofoam cup. "What number refill is that?" he asks me.

"First cup, actually," I tell him.

"Wow," he says. "I'm impressed. I've already had three of them and I've been in surgery since ten o'clock."

The elevator dings at the fifth floor and I nod. "Well, have a good day."

"You too, Eliza."

Apparently, I was not the only one scoping out the nametag. The door closes behind me and I shake my head as I swipe my badge and walk through the double locking doors.

"What?" Roseanne, one of the other nurses on the floor is looking at me from behind the desk.

"Have you ever dated a doctor?" I ask. Roseanne is one of the few single nurses on this floor. Like I said, the majority of my coworkers on this floor are either married with little kids or married with grown and gone kids.

She just starts laughing. "Girl, you do not want to go there."

"I figured as much."

"My dad was a doctor, you know. I know all about life with doctors. And let me tell you, the paycheck is nice but you trade it for time."

I nod. "Got it."

"My poor mother spent thirty of their thirty-two anniversaries by herself in a restaurant because Dad got called back in or didn't get off in time for dinner."

"That's sad."

"Yep. It's also the reason she filed for divorce and she's now married to a retiree who takes her on these extravagant vacations and does nothing but hang out with her while my dad is calling me up almost every night because he's finally realized that he missed dinner the entire time I was growing up and is trying to make it up now." She shrugs. "You can't make up everything, you know."

"I'm sorry, Roseanne."

She waves a hand. "Eh, it's all water under the bridge or over the dam or whatever. But my point is that you got to catch a man who has his priorities straight instead of his 401k all padded."

"Wise words."

"Ones I have to remind myself of often," she says, grinning. "Because I will say, there are some fine faces on top of those white coats out there. I need to learn how to cross-stitch so I can write those thoughts on a pillow and see it every time I get home."

I laugh and head to start up my rounds again.

I get home about eight o'clock after stopping for a quick dinner at Panda Express.

Here's the thing about Panda Express food: It always sounds great to me and smells great to me until the second I take my last bite, then it sounds terrible and smells awful. If by some weird fluke I happen to lave leftover orange chicken, I never take it home because the smell lingers in my car and makes me sick to my stomach for the next three days.

It's just this weird thing.

I rub my cheeks as I walk in the garage door. They already feel oily.

Might need to do like a de-greasing mask or something tonight.

"You okay?"

I jump about eight feet into the air at the voice and whirl, grasping for some sort of weapon to attack this intruder who apparently cares how I'm doing.

Ashten starts laughing. She's sitting at my kitchen table and there are papers and sticky notes everywhere. She's got her computer open in front of her. "Sorry. Didn't mean to scare you."

"Did I know you were coming over?"

She shakes her head. "No. Katie and Luke decided they wanted to try making homemade cinnamon rolls."

"Okay," I say slowly.

"Right? That's totally my thought too. Anyway, she found the recipe on some blog but apparently overlooked that it made like one hundred and fifteen rolls, so there is seriously flour and dough covering like every inch of the kitchen counters and the table." Ashten shakes her head. "And I have progress reports due tomorrow."

"Got it. Stay as long as you want."

"What do you think about Luke?" Ashten asks, playing with a pen and apparently trying to distract herself from progress reports.

I shrug. "I mean, I don't know him super well, but he seems like a nice guy. What do you think about him?"

"I think he's a good fit for Katie, but he kind of makes me insane."

I grin. "What do you mean?"

"I mean, he's so *cheerful*. It gets annoying."

I laugh. Ashten rolls her eyes.

"No, I mean it. I have never seen him get upset. About anything. A bag of flour exploded when they were in the middle of mixing everything and Katie like freaked out because flour was seriously everywhere. I mean, it probably got in the ductwork and we're going to be inhaling small flecks of flour for the rest of the year."

I grin. "Hopefully no one is gluten intolerant at Bible study then."

"Anyway, Katie's all freaking out about the mess and Luke is laughing and starts like throwing the flour in the air like it's snowing. He's a freak of nature. I mean, I honestly wonder if he has some sort of personality disorder where he doesn't feel sadness."

I'm still laughing. "Oh Ashten."

"What? It's totally possible. You know how there are those people who don't feel pain? He could seriously be one of those people who doesn't feel frustration."

"There are days where that would be a good disorder to have," I say, poking around in my pantry. I know I bought Nutter Butters, I just can't remember where I put them.

"Cookies are on the table," Ashten says.

"Nutter Butter Thief."

"Girl, you can't even imagine my day. I will pay you for the cookies."

I get myself a cup of decaf from the Keurig and grin. I'd offer Ashten a cup, but she doesn't drink hot drinks unless she's sick and even then, it's only tea.

It's amazing we are friends.

"So. What happened? Or do you need to work?" I judge the mess at the table and decide to sit on a barstool at the counter.

"We had a bathroom accident, then a kid legitimately lost his shoes at recess, I had a live lizard get into my class and I had three parents who wanted to talk about their kids come in after class. All at the same time." Ashten rolls her eyes. "People. This is why we set up parent/teacher conferences. Which are next week. But none of these parents are available during that time, apparently."

"So naturally, you're supposed to just be available anytime, then."

"Exactly."

"Sorry about that."

She sighs. "It's part of the job. Okay. Four more reports to go. I saved the easiest for the last, so I'll be out of your hair in just a bit."

"You aren't in my hair. Take your time. I'm going to go take a shower."

"I was going to say, you smell like hospital."

"You know, I'm so glad you live across the street so you can come over any time you want and eat my cookies and insult me."

She grins and crunches a Nutter Butter. "I love you, Eliza."

"Mm-hmm."

"You're beautiful."

I shake my head and slide off the barstool. "Backpedaling. Backpedaling while still eating my cookies." I head for the bedroom.

"Have a good shower."

Most of the time, I have to leave my house by six in the morning just to give myself a little bit of time to find parking and make sure I get there in time for a quick rundown from the night nurse.

So there is absolutely no way I am going to get up any earlier than I already have to so I can take a shower before I leave in the morning. I'm already up by five-fifteen usually, and that's because I like to wear eye shadow. I have coworkers who get up before five so they can get a shower in. Yeah, no thank you. Especially since I'll be taking one when I get home to wash all the germies off from the hospital anyway.

I'm out of the shower about ten minutes later and I dry off and then spray a good-sized dollop of mouse in my hands, rubbing them together before I run it through my hair.

My hair is far too long. I hold up the ends and study them. They are in terrible shape. I'd say a good ninety percent of the time, my hair is up in a sloppy bun, so I rarely notice my ends but it's definitely time for a cut. I don't think I've even had a haircut in the last six months.

That's just no good.

I blow dry my hair so it's good to go for my shift tomorrow, pull on my favorite pajama pants and a long-sleeve T-shirt and go back out to the kitchen. Ashten is now sitting on my couch, eating popcorn and turning on the TV to "Fixer Upper".

"Making yourself at home, I see," I say, getting myself another cup of decaf before I go join her on the couch.

"You smell better." She leans over and sniffs my hair.

"Um. Hello. Personal space bubble."

"What kind of shampoo do you use? It smells good."

"I don't know. I got it free from the hospital."

"The hospital gives out free shampoo?"

"It does when you leave it there."

Ashten grins. "You stole shampoo from one of your patients? Isn't that against the HIPPA code or something?"

"Okay, first off, HIPPA is not a code. It's a law. Second, I had one of the LPNs call them and see if they wanted us to mail it to them and they said to just toss it. But it was a full bottle, so I just decided that rather than throwing it away, I would put it to good use."

"Look at you, all thrifty."

"Only when it comes to shampoo."

I know it's a new thing to go to garage sales and spend the next two weeks basically rebuilding a nightstand into a five piece dining set using only stain and Gorilla Glue, but honestly? I'd rather just pay the extra five hundred dollars and buy a dining set all ready to go.

Pinterest and I are not very friendly.

Ashten, on the other hand, is totally crafty and creative. She's one of those people who drives a rental truck down to IKEA and comes back with all kinds of useless junk that she somehow turns into amazing, one of a kind pieces.

I believe the woman even owns a soldering tool.

That makes her basically on the same level as a carpenter in my book.

The couple on the TV are taking sledgehammers to what I think is actually a pretty brick fireplace. "What are they doing?" I ask.

"They're replacing it with stone. This show is seriously my favorite show on the entire planet. I would die to have them redo my house whenever I actually get one of my own."

"What are you thinking as far as that goes?" I ask, pulling a couple of Nutter Butters out of the package.

I swing back and forth on whether I like these or Oreos better. I've finally decided that it has very little to do with the actual cookie and more to do with what my day was like. Rough day? I need Oreos. Okay day? I want Nutter Butters. Terrible, awful day? I need homemade chocolate chip cookies and nothing else will suffice. I've substituted a Chick-fil-a chocolate chip cookie once and it was all right, but it was sort of to the same effect of your mom putting one of those flesh-toned band-aids on you when you really wanted a Hello Kitty one. It did its job, but that was about it.

Ashten finishes swallowing a mouthful of popcorn and shrugs. "I don't know. I really like living with Katie. But honestly, I bet she ends up marrying Luke."

"You think so?"

She nods. "They haven't said anything and really, I don't even know if he's officially asked her to be his girlfriend, but the writing is on the wall, friend. And it's now covered in flour."

I laugh. "Want to stay here tonight so you aren't breathing flour dust while you sleep?"

"No, I have to get up early to get some stuff ready in my classroom for the day."

"Probably not as early as me," I say. "I'm leaving the house at six."

"I would die if I were you. And the early mornings are just part of that reason. I don't see how you deal with blood all day long. Especially on such little sleep."

"You get used to it," I say. The man in the show just discovered a mold infestation throughout one of the walls.

Gross.

"I would never get used to it," Ashten declares. "God did not make me to be a nurse."

"I don't see how you deal with boogers all day long," I say. "I can't stand kids."

"They're more than just their boogers," Ashten grins. "And good grief, Eliza, you work with kids too."

"No, I work with newborns. There's a big difference and it's like no one understands this."

Other nurses get it. I've met labor and delivery nurses who can't handle babies, which is just bizarre to other people but makes total sense to me. A patient is a patient. And honestly, the babies are just extensions of their mothers for me.

They definitely aren't kids.

"Anyway," Ashten says. "To get back to your original question, I've actually started looking around this area for a house of my own."

"No way! That's great news. Maybe one of our neighbors will leave so you can live here on the same street."

She grins. "Wouldn't that be awesome?"

"It would. Let's start leaving stuff that smells really bad on our back porches so people will move. Or you guys can get a little yappy dog that makes everyone insane."

"Why don't you get the yappy dog?"

"I don't like dogs."

"Good grief. You and Katie. Katie thinks they are too messy."

"I just don't like them." I'm not sure why but I've never liked dogs. Mike likes to tell stories about how I would shriek in fear and climb up my parents' legs like a fire pole whenever a dog dared to come in my general vicinity.

It probably doesn't help matters that Mike is always forwarding me these awful stories of people attacked by dogs. He likes to feed into my fears.

We watch the rest of the show, commenting on the design choices and the color scheme. When the credits start rolling, Ashten looks at the clock and declares that it's bedtime.

"I love you, Eliza," she says, shouldering her bags. "I'm so thankful that we are friends. I'll see you soon."

"You're welcome for the Nutter Butters."

She grins. "And the popcorn. Thank you."

"Anytime." I mean it and she knows it.

"Night."

"Good night."

CHAPTER *Ten*

I work all day Friday and Saturday and by Sunday morning, I can barely open my eyes in time for church.

And I go to the late service.

I think this is how I am with work. I can work four twelves in a row but by the next day, my adrenaline has completely worn off and I'm pretty much useless for the entire rest of the next two days.

I drag myself out of bed, stumble to the bathroom and stare blearily at myself in the bathroom mirror.

People will probably witness to me at church today and tell me how Jesus can turn around even someone who lives on the street. I am in rough shape today.

I poke at my forehead. This is likely because I'm not the biggest fan of sunglasses, but I have legitimate wrinkles forming on my forehead and at the corners of my eyes. I'm thirty-one years old. If fifty is the new thirty, does that make thirty the new ten? Because the collagen on my face hasn't heard that news yet.

I scrub my face in the shower with the anti-aging stuff that promises to reverse time but as far as I can tell when I get out, the only time that needs to be reversed is the time I bought that bottle of anti-aging face wash.

I swipe on mascara, add a little eye shadow and then find a pair of jeans that are free of distressing. I don't know what it is, but there's just something deep in my soul that cringes at the thought of wearing distressed jeans to church. I have decided that at some point along the way, I must have gotten in trouble for wearing holey jeans to church. I can kind of hear my mother telling me that your jeans should be patched and your heart should be holy.

Or something like that.

I dig a silky pink shirt out of the closet, mourn over the curls that are already falling out of my hair, grab my Bible and head across the street. Katie usually drives us to church. I don't think there was ever an official agreement that she would drive us, but she does every week anyway.

Her garage is open and Ashten is already in the passenger seat. I slide in the backseat. "Where's Katie?"

"She couldn't find her lipstick."

"Oh."

"Yeah."

This is not a common theme. Katie is usually right on time, if not a few minutes early everywhere she goes. She is one of those annoying people who shows up when you're still trying to get dressed for the get together you are throwing, and I speak from experience.

Katie comes running out three minutes later and I guess she found her lipstick, because her lips are a nice corally color.

"Late. We are going to be late," she's grousing under her breath. She huffs her breath out in this little growl and then looks back at me. "Good morning, Eliza," she says, putting the car into reverse and backing out of the driveway. "Get any sleep last night?"

"Are you kidding? After four days on? I was basically asleep driving home from the hospital last night."

"Well, that's a comforting thought for your best friend. Thanks."

"No problem."

"Where was your lipstick?" Ashten asks.

"I guess it fell out of my purse somewhere. Probably on the last plane I was on. I found this buried in the back of my makeup drawer."

"It's pretty," Ashten says.

"Spring-y," I nod.

"It tastes like chalk, so this is the only time you'll ever see me in it," Katie says, making a face. "I think it was produced before that study that came out that said how many pounds of lipstick the average American woman eats every year and they started taking pity and making it at least taste decent."

Ashten's nose wrinkles up. "Ew."

"I know. The chalk stuff is gross."

"No, I mean, the *pounds* of lipstick. That's disgusting. I'm officially giving up lipstick."

Katie looks over at her. "Do you usually wear lipstick?"

"No."

"Is this like giving up liverwurst for Lent type of a thing?" I ask.

"Probably."

I laugh.

We get to church and find our usual spots in the middle toward the front. I love to sit in the front. I think it helps my ADD to be close enough for the preacher to make eye contact with so that if I start getting antsy, at least I know I'm being stared at by a man of God.

Katie, however, I think is a back row Christian, so we've compromised. There were a few weeks where I think she kept moving us back one row at a time and I finally caught on and we had a little chat about her front row insecurities and moved to the middle.

The music starts, we sing the first song and true to form, Luke comes in right about then. Compared to Katie's perfect punctuality, Luke is like the polar opposite. I've never seen him on time for anything and most of the time, he's a good ten or fifteen minutes late. I have no idea how he does this with the weddings he performs at. I would think that brides would be at his throat with a hatchet every week.

Our church has a very predictable rhythm of sing three songs, listen to the pastor speak for forty-five minutes, then sing one song and listen to announcements to close. We sit after the third song and one of our associate pastors who preaches every so often, Pastor Mark, stands up and goes to the pulpit.

"We are beginning a six week study in the book of James," he says into the microphone. "Most of our pastoral staff is in Ecuador for the remainder of this season as they equip pastors in our sister churches there and undergo training, so you get me for the next few weeks."

James again. Apparently, God is really wanting us to learn something in James.

And for the record, I just think it's weird when everything all lines up with what God is teaching you. I remember right after my mom died, it seemed like every single thing I did involved something from Romans 9. My church was studying it, my Bible study class with the youth group was studying it, my devotional book was studying it and then I kept getting cards in the mail with random verses from the same chapter.

I mean, don't get me wrong, it was definitely helpful and a great chapter to read when you have lost a family member. But it was a little creepy.

We open our Bibles to James and Pastor Mark starts reading in the first chapter, covering what we have been covering in Bible study and then going further into what we are reading this week for our study on Wednesday.

"My wife likes to tell me that part of the reason she married me is so that she can be an extra set of eyes making sure I'm not out in public with food on my face or something in my hair," he says. "When I was single, I was more or less a gigantic mess. I once went through an entire day in college with a Cheeto stuck to the back of my hair."

Ashten and I start giggling. Mostly because I can totally see Pastor Mark doing that. He's this goofy, kind of awkward, painfully thin guy who obviously loves Jesus and loves his church and it just makes you like him a lot. It's sort of like looking at a Golden Retriever puppy who's feet are just a little too big for it's body.

I'm not sure that's a compliment, but I really do like Pastor Mark.

"When James talks about being hearers of the Word and not doers, he uses this example," Mark says. "He says it's like looking into a mirror, seeing what you look like and walking away and totally forgetting. It would be like if you woke up, looked into the mirror and saw big, old drool marks all down your face, food all crusted into your hair, big, old boogers everywhere and you turned away and just thought you looked ready for the red carpet. No one does that, right?

We clean ourselves up. We change because of what we saw in the mirror. And sometimes, our job as fellow Christians is to follow each other around, holding up the mirror of the Word to each other."

I smile.

"James doesn't mince words," he says, closing his sermon a little while later. The margins in my Bible are filled with notes by this point. "We as modern day Christians need to take a few notes from James. He sees sin in his church and calls it out. He sees the need for encouragement in his church and he takes the time to speak truth into their lives. He wasn't politically correct, he didn't beat around the bush." Mark smiles a warm smile at the congregation and you can tell he just really loves this church. "We all could use a friend like James. We all need to be a friend like James."

We sing a song, listen to a few announcements and then church is dismissed.

The sanctuary bursts into the typical commotion of a bunch of people gathering their belongings and visiting over the music playing on the speakers.

"So, that was good and convicting," Ashten says, standing up next to me. "And we just studied that same passage. I'm amazed at how much we missed."

"I don't think we missed it as much as he just found different things than we did," I tell her. "But yeah, it was convicting."

"And now, I feel a little more prepared for Wednesday," Katie says, grinning. Pastor Mark did the section we are covering this week. "That was good timing."

"I've never thought about the mirror thing quite like that before," I say, flipping my Bible open again and making sure that I got those notes down legibly.

"Right?" Ashten nods. "I've always heard those verses about being a hearer of the word and not a doer and how it's like looking in a mirror and then immediately forgetting what you look like, but I've never correlated it like that."

Luke is nodding and smiling. "Great sermon," he says. "So what is everyone up to for lunch today?"

Ashten sighs. "I'm actually on my way to work," she groans. "Progress reports are killing me. We've got parent teacher conferences all week. So, I need to finish the last couple of report cards and get my classroom in order."

"Yuck. Sorry friend."

"Eight more weeks of school."

"Nice!" Katie smiles at her. "And you're working the summer at your grandparents' restaurant again, right?"

Ashten's grandparents own Minnie's Diner, which is apparently something of a local cult favorite here. People drive for hundreds of miles to visit and the restaurant, while it sounds like this little hole-in-the-wall, is actually gigantic. They even sell T-shirts with their restaurant logo on them and often sell out of them.

I feel like that's when you can honestly say that you've made it as a diner.

Ashten is nodding. "Yeah, I'm going to be starting there the Tuesday after Memorial Day," she says.

"You never stop, do you?"

"Not often."

"Well, do you guys want to go get lunch?" Luke asks me and Katie.

This is nice and awkward. As much as I love being the third wheel, I don't love it that much. "I need to do some stuff at home," I say.

I have no idea what I need to do but surely I need to do something. Laundry. I could always do laundry. Especially after four straight days working.

"Mind running us home before you guys go eat?" Ashten asks Katie, since she drove us here.

"Or, they can just drive your car back and I'll drive to lunch," Luke suggests to her.

Katie's cheeks are this pretty pink color and I can see what Ashten is saying as far as the writing on the flour-covered wall.

"Sure, sure," she says and digs around in her purse, handing Ashten the keys. "Just park in the driveway."

"Good grief. I knocked over the trash can once while parking in the garage. One time. That's it."

Katie grins. "You will never be trusted again."

"I know." Ashten rolls her eyes. "Go have lunch. I'll try to only knock down the recyclables this time."

"Thanks for the comforting parting words."

"No problem."

I grin and follow Ashten out to Katie's car. She's grumbling the entire time she puts her seatbelt on.

"One time," she mutters again and I grin.

"Y'all are just really enjoying this roommate thing, huh?"

"Just ridiculous," Ashten rolls her eyes again. "Anyway. I might go do my work at the diner. You're welcome to come for lunch, if you want."

"Is it not hard for you to work on school stuff there?"

Ashten shrugs. "I mean, sometimes it's distracting, but honestly it can be more distracting at home. That's why it was nice going to your house the other night. I didn't have my own laundry sitting there calling to me."

"You could have done my laundry," I tell her.

"No way, Jose. I don't do other people's laundry unless I'm related to them. And even then, it's a stretch. Have you ever noticed that every person does their laundry slightly different? Kind of like how no one makes chocolate chip cookies exactly the same way? It's like all of mankind is wired just weird enough so that nothing is ever the same, even if you are following the exact same directions."

"Proof of a Creator, I guess," I say.

"Amen."

We pull onto our street and Ashten parks in the driveway, grumbling again. "We couldn't just move the trash can, could we?"

I laugh. "Ah, the joys of roommates."

"Exactly." We climb out of the car and Ashten waves at me from the garage. "Sure you don't want to go to the restaurant?"

I never answered her but I guess she's taking my non-answer as a no. "Probably not," I say. Minnie's Diner is kind of a drive. And I need to do laundry. And probably watch *Gilmore Girls.* "I think I have some sandwich stuff."

"Okay. Well, you are welcome anytime."

"Thanks Ashten."

I walk across the street and I'm just pulling up the knob to start the washer when I hear a knock at the door.

I sigh. Of course someone is here now. I seriously *just* changed from my cute church clothes into my oldest and grossest pair of sweatpants and a shirt that I got at a breast cancer fundraiser when I was in nursing school. It says "CHECK YOUR BOOBIES" right across the chest. It's neon pink and it's a shirt that I am extraordinarily careful to only wear when it's laundry day and there is zero chance that I'm going to see someone of the human decent.

I walk to the front door and look through the peephole.

You have got to be kidding.

Cooper McClowski is standing at my front door, grinning all big-toothed into the peephole.

I open the door. "Did I know you were coming?"

He squints at my shirt. "Well, it's an interesting outfit choice if you knew I was coming, but thank you for the reminder. I'll be sure to check my chest area tonight when I get back to my hotel room."

I sigh. "It's laundry day."

"My favorite day!" Cooper says brightly.

"You are weird. What are you doing here?"

"Well, Lyzie, I made you a mixed tape."

I just look at him and he grins. "Wait, seriously?" I ask.

He pulls a flash drive from his jeans pocket. "Behold, the mixed tape of the two-thousand-teens." He frowns. "Teen-two-thousands? I'm not sure how to say this colloquially."

One of the things that I grudgingly have to admit that I actually like about Cooper is his vocabulary. And he's such a natural at taking

142

charge that it's no wonder he's climbing the ranks at the fire station. Last I heard, he was training to be a Captain.

I have no concept of firefighter ranks, but Captain sounds pretty high up there.

"So you drove all this way to give me a flash drive?" I ask him.

"Well and to see if you want to go get dinner with me. Though, I will have to insist you change before we go," Cooper says, grinning. He looks around my house.

He's totally here to check up on me.

I shake my head. "You could at least be more subtle about it. Did you and Mike draw straws or something?"

"What are you talking about?" he says, feigning a shocked voice. "I'm only here to see you."

"And the house."

"And your house."

"And to make sure there's nothing leaking or exploding or on fire."

"Well, I mean, I was hoping if something was, I would notice it. I am, as a matter of fact, a firefighter, so I know a few things about stuff being on fire."

"And I bet it has something to do with that guy I met at the gym too," I say.

Cooper grins. "Please. I'm just here to offer you the mixed tape and take you to dinner. I've had six different people over the last four months tell me about Minnie's Diner and how good it is here. Time to come try it for myself."

I close the front door in recognition that I will likely not be watching *Gilmore Girls* alone tonight.

I mean, it could be worse. And honestly, it's kind of nice to have the company. Especially company that gets me.

He's smirking and his dimple appears under the slight five o'clock shadow he has going on, eyes sparkling.

Cooper is a really nice looking man.

"Remember me telling you about Ashten?" I ask, changing the subject in my brain before things get all weird.

We are basically siblings.

We are basically siblings.

Sometimes I just have to repeat it a few times for myself. I think I just miss him more than I thought I would and it's making me think things and feel things that I would never think or feel otherwise.

Cooper nods. "Yeah, your teacher friend?"

"Her grandparents own Minnie's Diner. I think her grandmother is Minnie."

"Very cool!" Cooper leaves the family room and has no shame about going into my kitchen and checking under my sink.

144

"Would you like a tour?"

He pokes his head back out from the cabinet. "Can I check off the items on Mike's list so he doesn't get mad? When he gets mad, he yells and Lyzie..." He sticks his bottom lip out pitifully. "I'm scared of the yelling."

"You two are ridiculous."

"Words you've said often over the years."

"Where is his list?"

Cooper reaches into his pocket and pulls out a folded sheet of paper and hands it to me.

"Oh good grief," I say as I unfold it. There are at least fifteen things on here. "'Replace the smoke detector batteries'? We just did this!"

"Even so. I have a package of batteries in my truck."

"So much for moving out and taking care of myself."

"Come on, Lyzie. Surely, you know Mike better than that. You might need to move to Paris...and even then, I bet he'd just move there too so he could keep watching over you. Not that you could make it to Paris without losing your lunch a few times."

"Could you just let that die? And I don't need to be watched over," I say and then I bite my tongue to keep from saying more. It's like Mike thinks I'm not capable of being an adult or something.

Cooper watches me for a minute and nods. "Show me the house," he says. "It's a beautiful home. I really like how you've decorated it. But you've always had a good eye for this kind of thing."

"Thank you. Keep in mind that I didn't know you were coming. It might be messy."

He looks at my living room. "If this is your idea of messy, we have to stop being friends."

"Okay."

"Now that was just mean," he says.

I grin.

I show him through my little house and he is either very good at pretending to be enjoying the tour or he's truly excited about every detail of the place.

Either way, it makes something deep in my ribcage warm and soft.

"And you and Mike painted this house, right?" he asks, lightly touching a wall.

I nod. "Yeah, right after I bought it."

"It looks great. You guys did a great job."

"Thanks. Eventually, I want to upgrade the bathrooms. The previous owners did the kitchen but never made it to the bathrooms."

"That would be a good investment."

"And I'd like to add a deck." I open my screen door with difficulty, because it always sticks and point to my backyard. The backyard isn't large but it's not terribly small. There's a little patch of grass and a handful of little trees. One of them is an apple tree, but the squirrels got to all my apples before I could last year.

This year is going to be different.

I've done my research. And apparently, there are better ways to beat them to my crop other than just sitting out there with a ping pong paddle and scaring them away anytime they came near.

Thank goodness. By the end of the year, I swear they just laughed at me.

Cooper walks outside and inhales. "Man, it smells good here. So much better than my apartment."

"Cooper, anything smells better than your apartment."

"That's because Mrs. Traverson downstairs smokes like eight packs a day."

"Isn't your apartment a non-smoking one?"

"Yeah, but even if you stand in the designated smoking area, if you're smoking eight packs a day, you're going to be emitting all kinds of nasty stuff into the air just from your clothes alone."

"Gross."

"So where is this deck going to go?"

I point to the tiny little step outside my screen door. "I want to put it in here and have it kind of go along the side of the house. Not huge, I don't want it to take up too much of the yard. Just enough that I can put a little table and chairs and maybe a barbecue out here."

"Do you know how to use a barbecue?"

"It can't be that hard."

He grins. "I think that would look really nice. Be sure you use cedar. It naturally repels bugs. And make sure you stain it and seal it really good and you won't ever have to replace it."

"Ok."

"And I would cut it in a little here and add some extra two-by-fours for support under this area because the ground looks a little soggy. And then I would—"

"Cooper?" I interrupt.

"Yeah?"

"Do you want to build the deck?"

He grins at me, squinting in the sun. "That would be great, thanks. Not that I don't trust that you would get a good guy out here to build it, but I just trust me more."

"You're ridiculous," I tell him again. I smile. "But thank you."

"I'll be right back." He goes inside and comes back out a few minutes later with a gigantic beat up old metal toolbox.

148

"I think it might be time to replace that," I tell him. "Did you hit it with your truck?"

"Hey, now. This is Grandpa McClowski's toolbox. He gave it to me himself. Told me that I could fix ninety-nine percent of my problems with it." He grins at me. "Though, to be honest, it hasn't helped me too much in the girl department."

He rolls his sleeves up, opens the toolbox, digs around in the bottom and comes out with a can of WD-40 and starts spraying my screen door track.

I watch him work for a minute. Cooper is wearing slim cut dark rinsed jeans and a button-down shirt. I can see the muscles flexing in his tanned forearms.

Cooper is a good-looking firefighter. There is no possible way he has trouble in the girl department. I bet women have been trying to talk to him every single day of his entire adult life.

"Coop?"

"Yeah?"

"Are you dating anyone?"

He looks up at me and then gives my screen door another shot of the grease. "Nope."

I get the feeling that he doesn't really want to talk about it. Cooper is not one to use one word when he can use three hundred and twelve, so the fact that he answers with just the single word almost says more than anything else.

He finishes the door and caps the can. "Okay, so we can mark that one off," he says, grinning at me and suddenly the old Cooper is back. He pulls the list out of his pocket. "Well, that one wasn't even on there. You got one free of charge, Lyzie."

I smile. "Thanks, Cooper."

"Maybe you won't get a weight workout opening your back door now."

"My now-flabby biceps and I thank you."

He grins. "A hard to open back door is a safety hazard, Eliza," he says, and I hear Firefighter Cooper coming out in his voice. "All exits need to be easily accessed in the event of an emergency."

"Yes, sir."

"Okay, Mike says here that one of your bathroom faucets has a leak?"

"My bathroom faucets are fine."

"Apparently, one is leaking."

"You can go check them if you want."

He goes into the guest bathroom and then my bathroom. "Mike's eyesight has deteriorated over the years. Makes me nervous when he drives at night."

"You guys are like an old married couple."

150

"Someone has to be there to remind him to take his meds."

"Mike's on medication?"

"He takes vitamins."

"Vitamins aren't medication, Coop."

"Then why do they taste like it?"

I grin.

CHAPTER *Eleven*

Minnie's Diner is packed to the brim and overflowing into the sidewalk and parking lot on Sunday night.

I have changed into decent jeans that were finally dry right before we walked out the door and a white dolman-sleeved shirt. I can never decide if I like this shirt or hate it, which is why it was still clean in the back of my closet. Even now, standing on the walkway outside Minnie's, I still can't decide. The whole large-cut sleeve thing is just weird. But maybe it's cute?

I don't know.

"So, what about you?" Cooper asks.

I wait for the rest of the question, but he's busy looking at the flower bed next to the walkway.

"What about me what?" I ask.

"Are you dating anyone?"

"Um, yeah, no."

"Not even shirtless muscle dude?"

"Not even. Though, I saw him again and he's apparently a doctor."

"A doctor, huh?"

"Yeah. He was on the elevator with me at the hospital. Not sure what floor he's on."

"Interesting." The way he says it though doesn't convey a lot of interest and he's still staring at the flowers.

I look at the flowers too. Maybe they're some rare, exotic breed or something.

They look like just normal petunias, so I don't know what is so interesting about them.

"This place must be really good," Cooper says, changing the subject. "How much longer do we have to wait?"

We were told forty-five minutes about twenty minutes ago. "Twenty-five minutes."

"I'm starving."

"Me too."

I can only think of a handful of times when Cooper and I have stood there without having something to talk about. Once was right after his mom showed up at his high school graduation and Dad had just died. Once was when Mom got the diagnosis. And once was at her graveside. I remember just sitting there in one of the white, wooden folding chairs with the comfortable seats and just staring at the casket suspended above the open hole and thinking about how my mother was going to be in that hole.

Forever.

And by that point, I had cried so much that I couldn't cry anymore. So I just sat there. Mike was trying to be the brave kid who was taking the semester off of college to take care of his little sister and keep the household running and he was talking to our aunts and cousins and random family members who had come to the funeral, trying to be the good host. And Cooper just stayed sitting next to me as everyone else stood and went quietly to their cars after the service. We were supposed to go to a lunch at the church afterward but even the thought of eating made my stomach hurt.

So I sat. And Cooper sat. And we didn't speak one word for almost an hour.

When I look back over my life and think about some of the most meaningful things people have done for me, that one is at the top of the list. He didn't try to fix it and he didn't try to comfort. He just was there with me.

I wasn't alone.

This silence is not like that, though.

I can't put my finger on it but it's different. I don't like it. As much as I claim to be annoyed by his constant joking, I really need him to do some joking right now.

"So, how's work?" I ask and I'm immediately just frustrated with myself at the lame question. I've known Cooper for thirty years and this is the best question I can come up with?

154

He grins at me. "Same old Lyzie. Still can't deal with silence."

"It's just very rare when you're around. It makes me worry that you're about to tell me something terrible."

He smiles at me but there's something missing in the normal spark of his brown eyes. "Everything is fine."

"Are you sure? You seem...I don't know. You just seem different."

He stretches his arms up and then shrugs. "I don't know. Maybe I'm just tired. I worked four shifts this week."

"Four? I thought you were supposed to cap out at three." Contrary to one of my twelve-hour shifts, Cooper's are twenty-four hours long.

That's a huge difference.

"I am but we're a little shorthanded lately. One of my guys is actually in China adopting their daughter and one of the other Captains got hurt on one of his shifts, so I filled in for him too."

Something in my chest squeezes tight at the words *got hurt on one of his shifts.*

"You'd better not ever get hurt, Cooper McClowski."

He smirks. "Would you come visit me in the hospital if I did?"

"Don't even joke about it."

His eyes immediately soften. "I won't, Lyzie." Whether he means joking about it or getting hurt, I'm not sure.

Nothing can happen to Cooper. He makes me crazy but he's family. I've lost too much family to make light of anything like that. Cooper is one of the two constants in my life right now.

The buzzer starts going off in my hand and I nod to Cooper. We fight our way through the throng of people inside the doors and over to the hostess stand. "Cooper, party of two?" she asks us.

"Yeah."

"Right this way." We follow her through the maze of the restaurant and we end up in one of the side rooms that I would bet functions as an overflow room on the weekend. I know Ashten said that there are a few different rooms at Minnie's that groups can rent out for rehearsal dinners or company meetings. This must be one of them.

We sit at the small, two-person booth and Cooper looks around. There isn't one empty table in the entire restaurant.

"Okay, my hopes are officially up for this meal," he says. "I don't like to get myself worked up over restaurant food because it usually lets me down, but I have a good feeling about this place."

"Go ahead and get worked up. It's great."

"What is good here?"

Last time I came with Ashten for a quick dinner when Katie was in New York for business and I got the chicken and dumplings. Ashten talked me into them. I do not like chicken and dumplings

156

because the dumplings are usually squishy. I have no idea why people like half-cooked dough.

But the chicken and dumplings here were hands down amazing.

"I got chicken and dumplings last time," I tell Cooper.

His eyebrows immediately go up. "What? Eliza Wakeman got *dumplings*? What happened? Did you lose a bet?"

Cooper knows me too well.

"They were good," I say.

"This from the same girl who won't even eat French toast because it's too soggy."

"Actually, the French toast is pretty good here too."

"Okay, now I'm not convinced you're actually Eliza. Are you an alien life form who has taken over and is wearing Eliza's skin like a coat?"

"Gross."

"Exactly your previous thoughts on French toast and dumplings. If you start suddenly requesting sugar water, I'm going to have to find a weapon."

I grin.

The waitress comes by looking harried. "Good evening, welcome to Minnie's. What can I get you both to drink?"

"I'll have sweet tea," I say.

"Okay, now I believe you're Eliza," Cooper says to me. He smiles at the waitress. "I'll have a Coke."

"I'll be right back with those and some rolls."

"Thanks," we both chorus.

"You know, I saw this whole YouTube video where they showed how Coke can get rust off of car engines and clean the inside of toilets," I tell Cooper.

"That's why I drink it. It cleans out my insides."

I laugh.

"So, are you thinking you'll end up staying here?" Cooper asks.

"At Minnie's?" I smile, avoiding the real question.

"I mean, it's big enough that you probably could."

"I don't know, Coop."

"It seems like a nice town," Cooper says. "Quiet. The people I've met so far have been nice."

"It is a good town." I look at Cooper. "Are you planning on staying in St. Louis?"

"I don't know." He sighs and the tired look comes back into his eyes. "It's not the same as it was when I first started working with the department."

"Because you're now a Captain?"

"Maybe. We've had some bureaucracy stuff that happened and they ended up reorganizing the department. Too many lawyers and lawmakers have their elbows in our business."

"I mean, I know how much you love lawyers and lawmakers."

Cooper rolls his eyes. "It's to the point where I feel like we almost do more harm than good in an emergency."

"I'm sure that's not the case."

"I'm not sure that it's not." He shrugs. "Let's not talk about my work. I came here to check up on you."

"So now you admit it."

He grins. "Not that you aren't a fully capable adult."

"Mm-hmm."

"So what do you usually do on Sunday nights?"

The waitress brings our drinks and a basket piled high with sweet, golden hot rolls and a bowl with an ice-cream-sized scoop of honey butter.

"Holy smokes," Cooper says.

"Welcome to Minnie's," I say.

We slather our rolls with the honey butter and Cooper closes his eyes as he takes a bite. "Holy smokes," he says again.

"So as a firefighter, is that like the highest compliment you can give?"

He laughs.

Cooper pulls to a stop in front of my house about eight-thirty. I think the sweet rolls broke the weirdness and Cooper was his normal, light-hearted self through the rest of dinner.

The miracles of honey butter, I guess.

"Are you working tomorrow?" I ask.

Cooper nods. "Yeah, I am. The only reason I got today off is because it was kind of a safety issue for me to be working so much, so my Battalion Chief had someone from another district fill in."

"Sorry things are so stressful there."

"Like I said, it's just all the red tape." He shrugs. "I still enjoy the actual work. I'm still glad I became a firefighter."

"That's good."

"I'm just doing some research. Enough about my work. Are you working tomorrow?"

I nod. "Yep."

"I need to let you get to bed."

"You need to leave so you can drive home and get yourself to bed. Don't you start at seven too?"

He nods.

"You definitely need to head that way."

"Is this your way of kicking me out?"

"Yes."

He laughs. "Thanks for letting me come take over your Sunday afternoon."

"Thanks for fixing my non-leaking faucet."

He grins. "No problem."

I climb out of the car and he waits for me to go inside before he waves and drives off.

"So, is that him?"

I scream and jump back, whacking my elbow on the door jam.

Ashten is sitting at my kitchen table, grinning at me, sipping from a coffee cup. "Hi there."

"Okay, I'm going to ask this one more time. Where is my spare key?" I rub my elbow, wincing.

"So, is that him?" she asks again.

"Him who?"

"Him, the mysterious proposer?"

I roll my eyes. "You and Katie have totally romanticized the entire situation."

"So, it was him." She smiles all smugly. "He's cute."

"So, you date him."

"Somehow, I don't think he's interested in me."

"He probably would be when he finds out you're one of the few people alive on this earth who know Minnie's roll recipe."

She nods. "Well, I mean, that does up the ante in my favor. But even so." She grins at me over her coffee cup. "He's cute," she says again.

"Good grief, what were you doing? Watching through the window?"

"Pretty much, yes."

I shake my head. "You could at least have some shame over it."

"Why?" She shrugs. "I was curious. He's like this dark, mysterious figure brooding in your past."

"Seriously, y'all need to lay off the Hallmark Channel or something. Cooper is not dark or mysterious and he's definitely never brooded. I don't even know what that means. Doesn't it have something to do with chickens? Don't chickens brood?"

"So, his name is Cooper…"

I rub my eyes. "How long are you staying tonight? I have to be able to think and potentially save lives tomorrow morning at seven o'clock."

She swallows the last of her coffee and stands. "Okay, I'm leaving." She puts her cup in the dishwasher and grins all cheesy at me. "Thanks for the coffee."

"Mm-hmm. I've heard there are some real nice neighborhoods to live in across town. You might should look over there."

"I love you too."

I close the door after her and shake my head. Then I open the door again and search all over the porch. Where in the world is she hiding my spare key?

I lock the door, though it doesn't seem to do much to keep people out, and go down the hall, pulling on my pajamas and brushing my teeth. I climb into my bed and pull my Bible over, flipping it to James.

I pick up reading in the first chapter so I'm ready for Bible study on Wednesday.

Do not be deceived, my beloved brethren. Every good thing given and every perfect gift is from above, coming down from the Father of lights, with whom there is no variation or shifting shadow.

I frown. Someone wrote this verse on the inside of a sympathy card they sent after Mom died.

First off, I do not understand sympathy cards. I would have one hundred percent preferred to not get a single one. Just like I would have preferred if there had not been a lunch after both my parents' funerals. I mean, who even started that? Who decided, "Hey, these people have just been through the hardest thing they've ever walked through, let's make them go eat a feast and visit with a bunch of people not even fifteen minutes later?" The last thing I wanted to do was eat and see people.

I remember looking at the verse and wondering if they sent me the wrong card. Maybe this one was supposed to go to someone who had just had a baby, not someone who had just lost their mother.

But no, there was my name clearly written above the verse.

I pick up my phone and open the Bible app that has all the different translations on it. Whoever came up with this app is amazing. I look up the verse and the Message translation appears.

So, my very dear friends, don't get thrown off course. Every desirable and beneficial gift comes out of heaven. The gifts are rivers of light cascading down from the Father of Light. There is nothing deceitful in God, nothing two-faced, nothing fickle.

Does that mean that God taking my parents was a good thing?

Surely I am reading this wrong.

I turn off my bedside lamp, pull the covers up to my chin and stare at the dark ceiling.

"Jesus, why?"

It takes me a long time to go to sleep.

CHAPTER *Twelve*

Monday morning, seven o'clock, comes way too early.

I shove my purse into the cubby, straighten my badge and rub my eyes. I don't know what time I actually fell asleep last night, but it wasn't a good time considering when my alarm went off, that's for certain.

"Morning, Eliza."

"Hey." I nod to Heather, one of the nurses on the floor. She's obviously just getting off. She's yawning and getting her stuff out of the cubby.

"How was the night?"

"Busy. But when is it not? You know, I read an article about how we haven't had a population surge since the Baby Boom, but it sure feels like we are in the middle of one."

I nod. "I agree." I think a lot of it is we are a smaller hospital but we are the main hospital for obstetrics for the surrounding area. Unless you want to drive into St. Louis, you deliver here. Or at home, I guess.

I know one nurse who has told me she actually is in favor of home births. Every other nurse I've met has been one thousand percent against them. I think it's because we instantly are thinking of every case we've had where something unexpected went wrong and we had less than a minute to save the mama or the baby's life. Since we are here, we have the equipment, we have the manpower, we have the sterile environment. If they were at home, it would be a different story.

I'm sure a lot of it is my education coming out. And my professors made no qualms about their position on home births. Maybe if I attended a home birth, I'd have a different opinion, like this other nurse had done. But still. I think I would be so on edge about everything the entire time, that I would just end up sticking to my original thoughts, even if everything went exactly according to plan.

I'm taking over Amber's patients and I've already read through all the notes she took on everyone. I need to make my initial rounds. Three mamas, three babies. Amber has a note next to a first-time mom who had an emergency c-section that her birth didn't go like she had planned, so she was having a really hard time.

Ah, birth plans. We have girls come in who are so tied to their birth plans, they can barely look up from their notes to notice their baby is being born. It's tough because I feel like the idea of the "birth plan" has replaced the practicality of just letting God, your body and your medical team do their jobs. And when it doesn't go like you planned, I think it probably puts the mama at a higher risk for postpartum depression. But at the same time, I understand the need to have a little bit of control.

So it's a toss-up.

I start with the room at the end of the hall. Mom's name is Jenny and the NBM – newborn male – is Gene.

Not sure I've ever had a baby named Gene as a nurse. I've met men in their sixties and up named Gene. But never a baby.

I open the door and smile warmly into the room, going straight for the sink and scrubbing up to my elbows as I talk. The TV blaring some reality courtroom show where a couple is arguing in front of a judge. "Hi there, Jenny. I'm Eliza and I'm going to be your nurse today. How are you feeling?"

She turns the volume down on the TV. "Sorry, what?" she says.

"I'm Eliza, I'm going to be your nurse today. How are you? Feeling any pain?" I dry my hands with three paper towels and walk over to the bedside.

The baby is in his plastic bassinet and has the chubbiest cheeks I've ever seen on a newborn.

"I'm okay. I could use some more pain meds, though."

"Okay." I pull her chart up and see when she had it last. "How is baby Gene eating?"

She tears her eyes off the TV again. "Sorry, what?"

I feel like I'm a nuisance. "How's the baby eating?"

"He's fine."

Gene is sleeping, so I guess I'm going to need to come back when he's awake. I take the mom's pulse, blood pressure and temperature and check her fundal height. She barely acknowledges me, eyes glued to the TV.

Maybe this is a tense scene or something.

"Okay, well, I'll be back in a little bit." I write my name and number on the white board in her room. "Here's my extension, so call me if you need anything, okay?"

She doesn't answer. I close the door behind myself.

Well, that was fun.

The day doesn't get much better. The c-section mom spends most of the day crying and refusing to take her pain medicine because she wanted a medication-free hospital experience. My other patient seems like a decent person but she has about fifteen people coming in and out visiting all day long. The woman has friends to spare. And most of them have very strong opinions on everything in the room, including the baby and the way she holds him or breastfeeds or breathes.

I mean, I'm getting offended on behalf of the mom, though it doesn't seem to faze her.

By the time seven o'clock comes around, I have a splintering headache. I find a bottle of Advil in my purse and I take three of them on my way out the double locking doors.

I drive home and head straight for bed, even though my dinner was a granola bar about three hours ago. I'm working tomorrow. And then Thursday, I have the night shift, so I need to start banking up sleep. Most of the time, as weird as it is, the night shifts are requested by the other nurses first, particularly the ones who have children of their own. And honestly, the night shift nurses on my floor have a much slower pace than the day shift nurses most of the time.

I climb into bed, look at my Bible and decide to just read it during a break tomorrow.

"I'm taking a five," I tell my charge nurse about ten-thirty.

Debbie smiles at me, tension lines across her forehead and nods. "Get me a cup too, please."

"Caramel?"

"It honestly doesn't matter. Caffeine. That's all I want."

I nod and leave for the elevator. Our patient with the thousand visitors is still here. I just discharged the TV watching mother and a new mom is on her way up from Labor and Delivery.

I mash the button on the elevator for the lobby and go straight for the espresso machine line. The line isn't too long this early, but there are still about six people ahead of me.

"Well, good morning."

I turn around and it's Dr. Samuel Wilmington behind me. He's smiling and putting his cell phone in his white coat pocket.

"Hi," I say.

"Time for a caffeine break?"

"It's been a long morning."

"You work on Mother Baby?"

I nod. "You?"

"NICU."

Seriously. He's good-looking, he seems to be semi-nice, he's a doctor and not just any doctor, he's a doctor trying to save babies' lives.

And he really couldn't come up with a better pickup line at the gym?

You would think all he would need to do is say, "Hello. I save babies" and people would just go ahead and propose or something.

Maybe I've just been around Cooper too much lately.

Honestly, I'm kind of surprised we haven't met before since we usually care for the mothers who's babies are in the NICU. I see doctors there constantly.

"How long have you worked here?" I ask.

"Going on my second month."

Well, that explains it. I don't think I've personally had a NICU case that lasted longer than a few hours in about six weeks. Sometimes, babies who don't score well on their Apgar tests will need to be admitted to the NICU for supplemental oxygen, but usually they are back upstairs with their mothers within twelve hours. My last NICU case was a mama who delivered at thirty weeks and she was so anxious to get to her baby's bedside that we bent about every rule in the book and discharged her early if she promised to just sit in the chair by her son's bed and not move.

I sent one of our LPNs down to check on her a few times and she apparently didn't even leave her son's side to eat.

It's those mothers that keep me going.

"Did you just finish your fellowship then?" I ask.

Dr. Sam nods. "Yep. Did my residency in Los Angeles and my fellowship in Minneapolis. One of the doctors I worked with in Minneapolis is actually from Carrington Springs and recommended me for this job."

"How are you liking the small town?" I'm the next in line for the machine, so I grab two cups and decide what flavor I'm feeling this morning.

Caramel. No, mocha.

Maybe I can mix the two together. Cara-mocha.

"I like it," Sam says. "Carrington Springs is a nice town. And it's close enough to St. Louis that I can go there if I need the big city feel for a the day. How about you? Are you from here?"

I shake my head and fill my cup halfway with caramel and the rest of the way with mocha. "No, I'm from St. Louis." I fill the other cup with caramel all the way for Debbie.

Poor woman. I can't imagine being a charge nurse. It's like all the work of nursing without any of the fun. I think all they do is field complaints all day long. I think I would have lost my faith in the human race completely by this point if I were her.

"Well, have a good morning," I tell Sam, trying to keep the conversation short and as un-personal as possible. Other teen girls grew up on stories about Prince Charming and Disney Channel romances. I grew up hearing about how we need to "LIVE IN THE YELLOW", which is code for living as paranoid as you possibly can.

Mike has a way of de-romanticizing everything. I had several friends who went backpacking across Europe after they graduated high school. I even got invited to come with them. The day after I mentioned it to Mike, I came home to find a stack a good inch thick of papers on my desk and every single one of them was an article of a person who had died while backpacking, died while in Europe, been kidnapped while backpacking, kidnapped while in Europe and dear gracious, let's not even get started on the unforeseen horrors of the friendly neighborhood European hostel.

Needless to say, I did not go.

Once again, the girl in search of adventure was handed a roll and told to stop singing and sit down, preferably in a safe place like the library.

One of these days, I'm going to compile a list of people who died while reading on a sofa. Maybe then Mike will relax a bit and recognize that people die doing safe things too.

It will likely backfire and I will end up only allowed to read on a wooden chair.

"Hey, Eliza," Sam says, catching up with me as I pay for mine and Debbie's drinks.

I look up at him, pocketing my debit card.

"Are you free for dinner tonight?"

I blink and every excuse I can think of is gone. "Um," I say.

He grins. "Great! We can even go somewhere right around here so we aren't out too late. I'm working tomorrow too. How about Gina's at seven-forty-five? Does that give you enough time to change over shifts and leave?"

"Uh—"

"Perfect! I'll see you then!"

He swipes his card and leaves, going in the opposite direction of the elevator that goes to the Mother Baby and the NICU floor, probably so I'm not able to say no on the ride up.

Well, I guess if the handsome Dr. Sam is a bust, at least Gina's has good food. And it's a public place. And like I told Mike all those years ago, you rarely have an adventure without taking a little risk.

CHAPTER *Thirteen*

The plus of working until after seven is that you usually miss the rush at restaurants since most normal people eat dinner around five-thirty. Gina's isn't crowded at all when I get there a few minutes before seven-forty-five.

I look around, but I can't see Sam.

"How many?" The hostess asks me.

"Two."

"Are you still waiting for someone?"

Apparently, this hostess has some basic addition skills that still need to be learned.

I rub my forehead and wince. *Sorry.* My tolerance for things ends up in the negative most of the time after work.

"I don't think he's here yet."

"Would you like to go ahead and be seated?"

"Sure."

She leads me to a table overlooking the parking lot. "Your waiter will be right with you," she says, handing me a menu and setting another one across the table from me. "Enjoy your meal."

I open the menu, which is pointless because I already know what I'm going to get. I've only been here a handful of times, but they have the best creamy sausage and potato soup I've ever had.

"Hi there."

I look up and Sam is sliding into the chair opposite me. He's wearing black dress pants, a gray button down shirt and a tie.

A little different attire than he had on at the gym. And way different attire than I am currently wearing. My hair is back in a ponytail and I can't remember if I put on mascara this morning or not. At least I went boring with my scrubs today. I'm just wearing plain navy blue. It's always freezing on the Mother Baby ward, which makes no sense considering we are dealing with hormonal women and tiny newborns, so I've got a long-sleeve white T-shirt underneath my scrubs. Paired with my red sneakers, I feel like I should have a tattoo on my forearm that says "'MERICA".

All this to say, I look like a nice, well-dressed stranger picked me up off the street corner and decided to feed me a good meal.

"Welcome to Gina's," our waiter appears right as Sam opens his mouth to talk. "What can I get you guys to drink?"

"I'll take an iced tea," Sam says.

"Same," I nod.

"Okay. Are you ready to order your food or would you like a few minutes?" the waiter says, making notes on his notepad.

I look at Sam, who nods. "I'm ready," he says.

"Me too."

"Go ahead, Eliza."

"I'll have the sausage and potato soup," I tell the waiter.

"Breadsticks and salad?"

"Yes please."

"Got it. And for you, sir?"

"Lasagna."

"Breadsticks and salad?"

"Definitely."

The waiter clicks his pen. "Sounds good. I'll have that out in a few minutes." He leaves and Sam smiles across the table at me.

"Thanks for coming to dinner with me."

I decide to go the candid route. "Well, you didn't give me a lot of choice," I say.

He grins. "That was my plan all along. So, tell me about yourself, Eliza."

Ah, my least favorite four words, right behind "my catheter fell out". What exactly does "tell me about yourself" even mean? Where I'm from? What I believe in? What my family life is like? What I'm allergic to? What I dreamed about last night?

"Well, I'm a nurse," I say.

He grins. "Right. Got that one down. What made you decide to go the Mother Baby route?"

I shrug. "That floor was my favorite when we were doing clinicals in school. And I don't know. There's just something about caring for people who have just had the most life-changing thing happen to them while simultaneously getting to care for one of the newest people on the planet."

He nods.

"What about you? How did you decide to do the NICU?"

"I mean, it's a very similar story as you," he says. "I was actually originally considering either the Emergency Room or adult ICU and then we did a NICU unit when I was in school. One of the babies was a twenty-six-weeker and I spent the entire unit working with her. She had six surgeries and we brought her back to life four times. She stayed there for two hundred days and is now a healthy eight year-old. I never turned back."

I smile. "That's amazing."

"It's a pretty incredible job. And exhausting."

"I hear you there."

"I'm sure you do. That's one thing that I've really noticed over the years is just how dedicated nurses are. I've probably worked with hundreds of nurses between med school, residency and my fellowship and I can only think of maybe one or two who I felt like weren't competent for the job or didn't have their heart in it. You guys are incredible."

He's very complementive, this one.

The waiter sets a towel-lined basket full of hot, buttered, parmesan-dusted breadsticks in front of us and a huge bowl of crispy, primarily iceberg lettuce salad.

So, I know that iceberg is like the donut of the lettuce family, but after years of forcing myself to eat romaine lettuce salads, I have just decided that I like iceberg the best and I'll get my leafy greens somewhere else. Sometimes, I even add spinach to my smoothies.

I also sometimes add blueberry sorbet, but that's another story for another day.

Now comes the awkward part. I have no idea what Sam's thoughts are on faith, but I guess there's no better time than right now to find out.

"Can I pray for the food?" I ask.

He smiles. "Sure."

I duck my head down and pray a very short, "thank you for this food" type of prayer. Sam nods when I finish and picks up his fork.

"So, you're a Christian?"

I nod. "Yes."

"That's cool."

He doesn't mention what he thinks. I guess I might as well ask. If he's not a Christian, this will be our one and only date.

I had a lot of friends in high school who would date people even if they didn't believe in Jesus and it just led to a lot of heartache. One of the guys I went on a few dates with when I was a junior or senior was an atheist and it was just a waste of time. Mike pointed out to me that every single thing we did was approached from a different point of view. I remember talking to him about something as silly as recycling when we went on a date to play mini golf. The guy, Dan, was very passionate about it, because this earth was zillions of years old and we needed to preserve it for the zillions of years to come. He was all into Mother Nature needing our help.

I mean, I think recycling is probably a good idea, but more because God put us on this earth to take care of it, not because I think we'll be here for a zillion years.

"So, what do you think about Jesus?" I ask, because I might as well.

He looks up from his lasagna, obviously not expecting to dive into these sort of waters on the initial date.

"Um, well, I guess I haven't really thought too much about it," he fumbles, fiddling with his fork and folding and refolding his napkin.

"Well, maybe you should," I say trying to instill some lightness in my tone, even though I'm completely serious. I kind of feel bad for him, though. He likely was not expecting a theological debate on this date to Gina's.

The conversation is just awkward after that. We try to make small talk, but I can tell that he's trying his best to eat as fast as he can so the date can be over sooner. I've met my fair share of young doctors over the years. I am willing to bet that he was looking for a good meal and probably a one night stand.

"Well, it was nice to talk with you," Sam says as we stand from the table.

At least he's polite. "Nice to talk with you too," I nod. "Hopefully we will see each other around." Just not super often.

"Have a good night, Eliza."

"You too."

We go our separate ways. I drive home and walk into my house, just kind of expecting to see Ashten sitting at my kitchen table, but the house is empty. It's almost nine o'clock. My early-to-bed neighbors should still be up for a few minutes.

I head across the street and knock on Katie's door.

She opens it, wearing her pink and gray plaid pajama pants, a pink tank top under a gray hooded jacket and a pair of black plastic-framed glasses, hair in a ponytail.

She looks like an ad for Old Navy's loungewear section.

Katie is one of those classically beautiful girls and the fact that she's not married has basically made me lose all faith in mankind. She's kind, she's smart, she's gorgeous and she even matches when she's about to go to bed. If there's a different description of the perfect girl, I'm not sure what it is.

"Hey!" she says brightly, opening the door a little wider. "Come in! I came by earlier to see if you wanted to have a late dinner with us but you weren't home yet." She looks at my scrubs. "Did you just get home?"

I nod. "Yeah." I follow her into the house and Ashten is sitting on the couch in the family room, also wearing pajamas.

"Hi Eliza!"

"Hey," I plop down on the recliner. Shockingly, they are watching HGTV.

Katie and Ashten watch more home improvement shows than any people with a non-fixer-upper house I know of. You would think if they were such fans of these type of shows that they would be living in a house that needed some serious work. But Katie's house is gorgeous and I know she only moved in just a little bit before I did and nothing has been changed except for the paint color.

"Holy cow, look at the kitchen!" Katie says, sitting down on the couch beside Ashten.

"Right? I love that they went with the gray cabinets. It makes the kitchen look so warm!"

One of these days, I truly believe that painted cabinets will be like my grandparents' orange shag carpet. Trendy for awhile and then the disgust of the next half-generation. Then everyone throughout America will be sanding down their cabinets back to the original wood and restaining them that "horrendous" oak-colored wood stain that everyone is painting over right now.

It's the circle of life.

The show ends and Ashten looks over at me as a commercial comes on the TV. "So, working late?" she asks.

"Did you ever get dinner?" Katie asks. "I have chicken enchilada leftovers in the fridge."

"I ate, thanks." I debate telling them about the date and then decide to just go for it. They are my best friends, after all.

"So, I had a date tonight," I say.

Katie immediately clicks the TV off and they both just look at me. "What?" Katie exclaims.

"With Cooper the Cute?" Ashten asks.

"No, with a doctor from the hospital."

"What?" they both say in unison, mouths wide open.

I grin. "I should go surprise dates more often, this is actually kind of fun," I say. "Though, really, could we tone down the shock? I'm not that unattractive, right?"

"Eliza, you are beautiful," Katie immediately declares. "I'm not in shock over someone asking you out, I'm in shock over you accepting the date."

"Yeah, I thought you didn't do that," Ashten says. "And if you do, how come you keep turning down Cooper?"

"Whom I still haven't met," Katie adds. "Very rude, if you ask me."

"It's not that I'm against dating," I say.

"Really." There isn't a lot of belief in Ashten's tone.

"Really," I insist. "Trust me, I would love to meet someone. And this guy was nice. I've seen him around a few times. But I found out tonight that he wasn't a Christian."

Katie nods. "Ah."

"I mean, his salvation status can change," Ashten says.

"I'm not sure he's anywhere close to that change," I tell her.

"Bummer."

"Was he at least nice looking?" Katie asks.

I nod. "Yeah."

"As nice-looking as Cooper?"

I roll my eyes.

Katie sighs. "I'm so sad that I missed seeing him the other night. Ashten said he was super dreamy."

"Ashten watches too many romance movies."

"What movies? I watch 'Fixer Upper'!" Ashten smirks at me. "Just go ahead and admit it. Cooper is really attractive."

I think it is a rite of passage that if you have a brother who is semi-close to you in age, you find yourself attracted to his friends. From what I've seen, this stage usually hits around fifteen or so.

So, yes, when I was fifteen and Cooper was nineteen, I remember thinking he was pretty cute.

And we did a few things that some would probably consider dates through the years. He took me to my prom, actually. Mostly because Mike wouldn't let me go with anyone else. And all my friends about died that a boy who was graduating college was there with me.

But I think about Cooper and he's just...Cooper.

"I mean, I guess he's nice-looking," I tell Katie and Ashten, since they are obviously waiting for me to talk.

Ashten immediately rolls her eyes. "Please. Katie, he's gorgeous. Like, picture a dark-haired Captain America."

"You have lost your mind," I tell Ashten. "He doesn't look anything like that. Like, not even remotely."

Katie sighs. "So bummed I missed him," she says, completely ignoring me.

"If you hadn't, then you'd know that Ashten is totally misrepresenting him," I tell Katie.

"So, you describe him," Katie says.

I open my mouth and then close it. "I don't know," I say finally. How do you describe someone you've known your whole life?

"He's tall," Ashten says.

I nod. "Okay, that part is true."

"And he's got this super thick, dark hair," she goes on.

Katie looks at me. I sigh. "His hair is brown, yes."

She grins. "This is painful for you."

"You guys just can't seem to get that he's basically like my brother. I seriously have pictures of this guy holding me when I had just gotten home from the hospital after being born."

Ashten shrugs. "But he's not your brother."

"But he basically is. It's just too...too..."

Both of them just look at me, not helping me at all.

"Weird," I finally say. "And predictable. Growing up, my parents both told me that they thought I would end up with Cooper. It's like *Little House on the Prairie.*"

"Well, I think it's romantic," Ashten declares. "It's like Emma and Mr. Knightley."

"See? Too many syrupy movies," I tell her.

"Whoa," Ashten says, sitting up straight and holding up her hands. "You can insult a lot of movies, but you may not insult *Emma*. No, ma'am."

"I'm on Ashten's side with this one," Katie says. "*Emma* is a classic."

"I wasn't insulting *Emma*, I was just pointing out that Ashten thinks this is romantic because of a movie," I say, trying to defend myself. "Trust me, I don't insult Jane Austen."

"Good," Katie says.

"Good," Ashten echoes.

"So, isn't Cooper the one who has proposed to you multiple times?" Katie asks.

I sigh. "Yes, but you guys have to know, Cooper is pretty much constantly joking. He would probably crawl in a hole and never come out if I'd ever said yes to one of his proposals. It's like his thing now. He sends me an email and ends it with a proposal. I don't think he has ever intended it as an actual marriage proposal."

"You don't think or you don't know?" Katie asks after a minute.

"Oh my gosh," I say, getting fed up.

"Look, all we're saying is that maybe Cooper really does mean something from all this. I mean, he's still single, right? Is he a Christian?" Ashten demands.

"Yes."

"So, he's gorgeous, he's single and he loves Jesus? What is wrong with you, woman?"

I rub my face with both hands. "You guys just don't get it. I have spent my entire life...my *entire* life surrounded by people who think they know what's best for me. Mike is constantly telling me what to do and Cooper is not that different. They always think they know what's best and if I even think about doing something different than how they would do it or if it's something that they aren't one million percent certain is safe, I basically get bombarded with lectures and articles and one thousand reasons why I should immediately reverse my course. You guys should have seen them when I announced I was moving. And I only moved an hour and a half away!"

Katie and Ashten are quiet, finally listening to me.

"All my life," I say quietly, rubbing my cheek. "All my life, I've just wanted to be my own person, away from Mike, away from Cooper, away from all the things that happened when I was growing up. I just want to have an adventure and know that it was *my* idea. Not theirs, not anyone else's. Just me. I don't want to be predictable. Seriously, like the worst thing I can think of someone saying about me is that I was predictable. I want to experience things and learn things and see things that I've never seen before. It's part of why I got a job where I only have to work three days to be considered full time."

"Do you think that part of Mike's reluctance to let you live independently is because of your parents?" Katie asks quietly.

"Oh, I totally think it's because of that. He's terrified that I'm going to die too, but you know what?" I pause, searching the air. I'm having trouble putting what I'm thinking into words. "I just feel stifled. I feel like since Mom and Dad died, my ability to live life has been taken away too. And I don't understand." I can feel the inside of my nose start to sting as the tears build behind my eyes. "I don't understand how James can say that every good gift comes from above when Jesus gave Mike and I the 'gift' of being orphans. I don't understand why God would think it was such a good idea to take Mom and Dad when He knew how hard Mike would take it."

The tears are spilling down my face now and without a word, Katie and Ashten are suddenly beside me, kneeling next to the chair and wrapping their arms around me.

"I don't even hardly remember my dad." I backhand my face and Katie hands me a Kleenex.

"I'm so sorry, Eliza," Ashten says. "I wish I had the answers."

Katie just smoothes my hair back from my face, not offering suggestions, but just offering comfort.

I sit there for a few minutes, gathering my thoughts and shrug. "Well. This is probably just all because I'm exhausted. I need to go home and go to bed."

"Sure you don't want to stay? I can make ice cream sundaes and we can watch a movie or something," Katie says, as I stand.

I shake my head. "Thanks guys. Soon."

I walk out the door, across the street and into my quiet, dark house. I turn on the living room lamp and sit down on my couch, pulling my knees up to my chest.

I sit that way for a long, long time.

CHAPTER *Fourteen*

Wednesday night, Katie's house is packed.

Completely, one hundred percent packed. We are going to need to relocate this Bible study as soon as possible.

Poor Katie is totally frazzled. She's trying not to show it, but I can see the frantic look in her eyes. People are sitting two to a couch cushion and every single square inch of the living room floor is taken ten minutes before the study starts.

Katie tells two people to please get off the kitchen counter before she pulls me into her bedroom.

"We have *got* to find a new place!" she hisses.

"I'll find one this week," I promise her. I would suggest my house, but we have the exact same layout. So unless we split in half, there's just no point.

Maybe we can meet at the park in our neighborhood during the summer. Daylight Savings just happened, so it's staying lighter out later.

We might all get eaten alive by mosquitos, but I guess we could talk about how we are going to consider those bites remembrances of what we've learned.

With every scratch, we remember.

And maybe we could just wear bug spray.

"How about the park?" I suggest.

"What park?"

"The one right around the corner? We could just go to Goodwill and get a bunch of blankets and people could just sit around on the blankets."

"That's not super hippy-ish?"

"Oh, it's totally hippy. But that's so in these days! We could be like the hobo Bible study people."

Katie is thinking about it, her forehead creased. "What about bugs?"

"We can spray the blankets with that citronella stuff."

"What about it getting dark?"

"We'll figure out something else when Fall comes."

"What about snack?" Every week, we make some sort of snack. Sometimes other people offer to bring it, but usually, it's just easier if we do it. Every time I'm at the grocery store, I pick up a package of those little appetizer-sized paper plates, plastic utensils and napkins for Bible study. Ashten and Katie usually do the baking.

"That's why they invented picnic blankets. Come on, Katie. You know you like the idea."

"I love the idea."

"So, let's do it! We can at least try it for a few weeks. If it doesn't work, we'll figure out a different location."

Katie nods. "Done."

Ashten pokes her head in the room and I can hear the not-so-dull roar of the people from the living room and kitchen. "Are you guys hiding?" she asks.

"Yes," Katie says.

"No," I say, rolling my eyes. "We are thinking we might move this thing to the park around the corner next week."

"That would be good. I think the couches are at their max weight capacity right now."

"If they break my couch, they are buying me a new one," Katie says. "And those are from Pottery Barn."

"I'll share the warning." Ashten clicks the door closed.

"Well, let's go," Katie says. She's obviously trying to psyche herself up for this.

"Remember, this is a good thing," I tell her.

"Oh I know. Kind of."

I laugh.

We walk back into the living room. I squeeze through the crowd and find my Bible underneath a rather large guy who is wearing glasses and a rust-colored shirt that says "C-3PO IS MY SPIRIT ANIMAL".

So much for the universal sign of saving a chair. But maybe C-3PO wasn't super observant. I'm not sure. I haven't seen the *Star Wars* movies more than once each and it was a long time ago.

In a galaxy far, far away.

I need to go to bed.

I dig my Bible out, stick my fingers in my mouth and whistle as loud as I possibly can.

The noise level immediately dies down.

"Everyone find a seat!" I say as loud as I can. "And while you're doing that, we have an announcement to make. We have outgrown this house."

Everyone kind of chuckles because it's the most obvious statement I could have made other than maybe saying that I am standing up.

"We are officially moving this study to the park around the corner. I believe it's called Wallace Park, but I will look it up and put it on the Facebook page. If you know anyone who isn't on the Facebook page who comes to this study, please let them know because we will not be here next week. Bring a blanket and Zyrtec because we will be sitting on the grass. If you are allergic to the sun, bring an umbrella."

More chuckling.

A couple of months ago, I got sick, Katie was out of town and Ashten was working at the restaurant, so we had to cancel Bible study.

Only, we had absolutely no way of getting ahold of everyone because it really became like this completely because of word of mouth. There are about twelve nurses I work with who come, a bunch of Ashten's teacher friends, some people from church and then they all invited people and those people invited people and now, there's at least five new people every week. So, we finally got smart and made a Facebook group so we can at least give most people a heads up if we have to cancel, rather than just sticking a note on the front door.

"So. next week, don't come here. Go to the park. Lots of parking, lots of space, lots of bugs, so bring bug spray."

A few more people quietly walk in and sit down in the entry way.

Apparently I will be making the same announcement at the end of the study.

"Everyone turn in your Bibles to James," I say.

Ashten is actually leading this week's discussion. The three of us take turns but occasionally, Luke will lead too. It's more just keeping the bunny trails to a minimum and asking good questions.

"Okay," Ashten says, when the flopping of the Bibles and crinkling of the pages dies down. "James 1. We're going to start in verse twenty-two." She clears her throat and starts reading. "'Prove yourselves doers of the word, and not merely hearers who delude themselves. For if anyone is a hearer of the word and not a doer, he is like a man who looks at his natural face in a mirror; for once he has looked at himself and gone away, he has immediately forgotten what kind of person he was. But one who looks intently at the perfect law, the law of liberty, and abides by it, not having become a forgetful hearer but an effectual doer, this man will be blessed in what he does.'"

She nods to me. She had asked me beforehand if I could read the passage again in a different version. "This is from The Message translation," I say. "'Don't fool yourself into thinking that you are a listener when you are anything but, letting the Word go in one ear and out the other. *Act* on what you hear! Those who hear and don't act are like those who glance in the mirror, walk away, and two minutes later have no idea who they are, what they look like. But whoever catches a glimpse of the revealed counsel of God—the free life!—even out of the corner of his eye, and sticks with it, is no distracted scatterbrain but a man or woman of action. That person will find delight and affirmation in the action.'"

"Thanks Eliza." Ashten looks around. "All right, so let's start the discussion off by looking closer at that first verse. We are talking about not just being hearers, but doers. What does that look like practically?"

"I mean, I think the obvious answer is that we don't just listen to what the Bible says and then walk out the door and keep living our regular life," one girl, I think her name is Brittany, pipes up.

"Right," Ashten nods. "But I mean, what *exactly* does that look like? Like, tonight, you guys all are going to walk out of here and get in your cars and what?"

"Drive home?" someone says hesitantly.

"Drive the speed limit?"

"Use my blinker?"

Ashten starts laughing and I grin.

"I mean, yeah," she says. "That's what I'm looking for. Basically, what are you doing that is not something that Jesus has told us to do?"

One of the guys who has been coming for a long time, Randy, raises his hand, which is totally unnecessary considering how most people just jump in and he knows that. "I'll tell you something I'm doing that I shouldn't be doing," he says.

I think we all get a little worried. Randy has said some bizarre stuff before, stuff that has made us contemplate asking a true pastor or counselor or someone with some training to come sit in on our not-so-little study. "What's up?" Ashten asks and I can hear the caution in her tone.

"I leave dishes."

"I'm sorry?" she says.

"I leave dishes. Like everywhere. I'll leave cereal bowls in my room. Or coffee cups. I'm really bad about leaving coffee cups. Sometimes I'll get my plate or fork or whatever to the sink, but I usually just forget and leave it there."

"Haven't you run out of dishes by this point?" another guy asks.

"I'm not sure that's exactly something that Jesus has talked about," Ashten says. "I mean, it's lazy, sure, and it's not very health-conscious, but you aren't really hurting anyone other than yourself."

"Well, see, that's the thing. I still live with my mom."

There's a collective *ah* and I think we all understand Randy a little more. I make a mental note to get the man a copy of *Failure to Launch* and perhaps a book on how to grow up.

Peter Pan has seriously ruined my generation of men. I think we can probably point the finger at a lot of different things leading to this mentality in men these days, but at the end of the day, dude, you just need to put the sippy cup down and put on some non-Velcro shoes and be an adult.

"So, your mom cleans up your dishes?" I can tell Ashten is having trouble even saying the words.

"Right. And she's mentioned it's annoying."

"Well, yeah."

"So, that's probably what I need to focus on."

Oh, Randy. Your focus needs to expand to more than just the dishes, but I keep my mouth closed. Surely, there is a guy about his age here who can pull him aside and remind him of his civic duties or something. I mean, I would say something, but I feel like it's not really my place.

But dear goodness. Randy's mother needs to have a talking to as well.

"So, um, does anyone else have any ideas?"

Poor Ashten.

I rarely talk here. If I'm going to share something, I usually just share with Katie and Ashten later. So despite how much I want to help her out, I stay quiet.

Thankfully, there are lots of other people here and the conversation is immediately picked back up and Ashten is saved.

A few people chime in about different things like actually listening when people are talking instead of just nodding and moving on or holding the door for people. Ashten is listening to all the comments and there's a slight line forming by her lips.

"Guys," she says finally after one girl says something about saying "please" and "thank you". She looks around at everyone. "Did you guys notice that almost everything that was mentioned was just simple courtesies? I mean, that's all great and all, but I really think

Jesus came to this earth for more than just teaching people to be kind."

Katie and I are nodding, as are a few people in the crowd.

"I mean, don't get me wrong, you should definitely say please and hold the door and drive the speed limit. But people do that who don't love Jesus. What did He *say*? How did He say it? How can we live it?"

You can almost hear people's brains popping from the sheer thought happening in the room.

"He said to love your neighbor," I say.

Ashten snaps and looks at me. "He said to love your neighbor," she repeats. "So basically everything we just mentioned can be shoved into that column. What else?"

"He said to love God and keep His commands," Katie says, clearing her throat.

"Right. And just so you know, His commands fill the entire first half of this book," Ashten says, holding up her Bible. "Don't murder. Don't steal. Don't look lustfully at people. Don't act on those temptations. Don't be unfair. What else?"

Now people are getting it and the sounds of pages turning fill the room as people go back to the Gospel stories to reference them.

I smile. You can feel the thought processes shifting in the room, you can see the lights turning on. This I love. You can just feel Jesus working in this tiny, overcrowded little house.

"He said to let your light shine."

"He said to not make His Father's house a place of business."

"He said anyone who believes in Him has eternal life."

"He said His Father has everything under control and it's for our good."

I remember when Dad died, it was just a shock to everyone. Our whole church was at our house for like an entire week. And people kept hugging me and bringing disgusting casseroles and hugging me and making coffee and hugging me and telling me every Christian platitude in the book while also keeping me from any possibility of time alone to process what had happened.

Romans 8 was a favorite of everyone who came. "And we know that God causes all things to work together for good to those who love God, to those who are called according to His purpose." I heard that quoted about forty-two times a day from women who crushed me to their chests and then gave me a potato chip and chicken casserole.

Then Mom found out she had cancer and we got more food. Macaroni salads and frozen lasagnas and enough flowers to start our own floral business. We got books on how to beat cancer and essential oils and ninety percent dark chocolate bars because they heard the antioxidants would fight the cancer.

And people would hold our hands and put their arms around our shoulders and tell us that God had a plan for our good.

And Mom died almost exactly a year later. After she wasted away to less an a hundred pounds and Mike and I had to watch the whole thing.

It was not good.

It took me a long time to go to church after that. And to pray after that. And to breathe after that.

Sometimes I wonder who I would be if Mom and Dad hadn't died. Would I still have become a nurse? Would I have moved to Carrington Springs? Would I have been so anxious for something different?

I guess there's really no way to know.

I listen to the other answers people are throwing out and I can feel the old, familiar itch deep in my stomach, simmering in my joints, aching in my knees.

I needed to just leave.

CHAPTER *Fifteen*

Friday morning, I get home from the night shift at about seven-forty-five in the morning. I'm starving. I do a random night shift probably once a month and it always throws my body for a loop on what time it is, what meal it is supposed to be. I've gotten into a good rhythm for night shifts, but still.

I grab a yogurt and a peach and head into my bedroom for a nap. If I can get a four-hour nap in now, I should be able to get to bed at a good time and then I'll be back to normal tomorrow. I do not see how my friends who work the night shift and still have their own kids do this.

I've decided they are like superheroes who just don't sleep.

I wake up to my alarm at noon, take a shower and decide to just let my hair air dry. Whenever Ashten lets her hair air dry, it gets all curly and beautiful. My hair stays straight, but just gets limp and flat. But I've got the next three days off, so I'm not planning on doing much with it beyond pulling it back in a braid.

I dig my suitcase out of my garage and unzip it on the bed.

Time for a little outing.

I think I'm just stressed out. And tired. And it's making me dredge up all these memories that I've kept pushed down for so long and hidden behind a door in my heart so I could laugh and talk and pretend that nothing was wrong.

I toss a couple of T-shirts in the suitcase and a couple pairs of jeans. And a casual dress. Mom loved dresses. She said a good dress was the most versatile thing in your wardrobe.

I disagree, I tend to be more of a jeans girl. But still. There's something about packing. Anytime I start pulling out clothes, I always hear her voice in the back of my head reminding me to pack a dress and an extra pair of socks.

Not that I or my mother would wear the two of them together.

Twenty minutes later, I'm ready to leave. I text Katie and Ashten so they don't panic, toss my suitcase in the backseat and back out of my driveway.

It takes me all of about ten minutes to get to the highway and it's a straight shot from there. I'm cranking up the radio, trying to forget how long it's been since I visited.

An hour and a half later, I'm turning right off the exit. There are trees in bloom everywhere. We've had a late spring this year, everything is still budding and blooming and it's the end of March. I'm hoping that doesn't mean a late summer and a late fall. Late summers are miserably hot.

I pull to a stop alongside the curb and just sit in my car for a few minutes, looking around.

Flowers in little vases are covering the green grass, in uniform lines, back and forth, back and forth. The only variance is the flowers themselves – every bouquet is different, unique. Some have a spring theme going. Some have Easter colors with little bunnies poking out of the bouquet.

There are trees scattered throughout the cemetery and lining a lot of the roads and the entire perimeter. Mom always thought this was the most beautiful cemetery in town, so when Dad died, there was no question where she wanted to bury him. I remember sitting at the funeral director's office, listening to Mom describe what she wanted on the dual headstone for both of them, since she decided she would just go ahead and buy her plot too.

I take a deep breath, grip the steering wheel and then open the door, stepping out. Birds are chirping, the weather is perfect, there is barely a breeze. I step over the curb and onto the plush grass, walking along the lines of vases and careful not to step on any headstones.

There's a landscaping crew here today in the far distance. I can hear the slight whir of a couple of weed eaters.

I wonder what it's like to be a landscaper at a cemetery?

I walk the paths and things have changed a lot since I was last here. New, shiny headstones are lined up where there used to just be open fields. The trees are bigger, fuller.

I think I instinctively slow down as I get closer.

It looks like Mike has been keeping the flowers nice. That's good. I was worried it would be the same bouquet that was here the last time I came.

When was the last time I came?

I stop in front of the headstone my parents share.

William and Lorraine Wakeman.

The dates of their births and deaths are underneath their names. They had to add Mom's date of death when she died. It completely weirded me out when we would come visit Dad's grave when Mom was still alive to see her name and birth date on there. It was like she had one foot already in the grave. And then when we found out she had cancer, it just became this horrible reminder that the day was coming. And the more weight she lost, the closer I knew it was coming. Sometimes I wonder if she didn't fight as hard since Dad wasn't here.

Then I just feel guilty for assuming that.

Mom had gone back and forth and back and forth on what she wanted to engrave on the headstone and it was just their names and dates for a long time. Then, right before she died, she called the funeral home without me or Mike knowing and told them what she wanted engraved. I didn't even see it until the day we buried her. It was a chorus from one of her new favorite songs.

What a foretaste of deliverance

How unwavering our hope

Christ in power resurrected

As we will be when He comes

I look at the words now and kneel down and gently brush some blades of grass off the wording.

Mike had put fake blue hydrangeas and white baby's breath in the vase. They aren't faded, so I know he's been here recently.

I never know what you are supposed to do at graves.

Do I talk to them? It's not like they are here, they can't hear me. Do I stand quietly? Kneel out of respect?

I look at the headstone and it's shimmering bronze in the sunlight. I like that it's bronze and not silver or white or engraved rocks or something.

I take a deep breath.

"So."

I say the word out loud and I immediately feel silly. Even when I lived in St. Louis, I rarely came here.

Too many memories. And not good ones.

I feel the grass with my hand and it's not wet, so I sit down and pull my knees up to my chest.

I came here a few times with Mike right after they died. We would come and stand and watch how quickly the grass filled in over their grave. It took no time at all and maybe it's because Mom died in the spring, but it was just a few weeks before you couldn't even tell that someone had recently been buried there.

If only hearts moved on as fast as grass grew.

I remember it was months before I could walk into our apartment without expecting Mom to be there or be half-waiting for the door to open and her walk in. Every weird creak, I would look up expecting her. She'd moved us into the apartment after she got the diagnosis and I think it's because she knew. She knew and she didn't want us have to sell the house and go through their belongings.

So she did it for us. She did it so gradually that I didn't even notice but after she died, Mike and I went in her room and found just two large plastic storage tubs in her closet, one labeled *Michael* and one labeled *Eliza*. Other than her few clothes, she had nothing else.

It took me a long time to open the tub, but it was full of all my special awards and belongings and a few just random papers. At the top was an envelope addressed to me in her handwriting.

I look at the gravestone. "I still haven't read it, you know," I say quietly.

I couldn't. I don't think I'll ever be able to.

I never asked if Mike opened his, but I know he had one too.

There are a few other people visiting the cemetery and I finally stand. It's just weird. Do I say goodbye? Do I wave? Salute?

I sort of nod my head and walk back to my car, being careful to walk along the path and I climb into the driver's seat and just sit for a minute.

It's Friday at four-thirty in the afternoon and I'm going to be stuck in traffic for awhile, but he might be home.

I find an empty parking spot almost an hour later. His truck isn't here and I start worrying that maybe he is working tonight. I walk around the back of the apartment building and go sit on the second stair from the bottom for the staircase leading to the upstairs apartment.

About twenty minutes later, I hear footsteps coming and I put my phone back in my purse. He comes around the corner and stops and a grin six-feet across spreads across his face.

"Eliza."

"Cooper."

He pockets his keys and pulls his sunglasses off his face, still grinning. "So, did I know you were coming and I just went to run errands because I'm a terrible loser, or is this a big surprise?"

I smile a close-mouthed smile at him. "Surprise."

He reaches a hand out and I let him help me off the step. "Best kind of surprise. Have you eaten dinner?"

I shake my head. "Nope."

"Let's go get something to eat. What sounds good? And I know why you are here." He grins at me, all big. "You listened to my mixed tape."

"Please don't remind me of the mixed tape." It was like he compiled an hour and a half of the most annoying songs of the eighties and nineties all onto the same flash drive. I couldn't get the Macarena out of my head for like three straight days.

I wasn't hungry until just this minute, but suddenly, I am starving. "And anything sounds great to eat."

"Pizza? Barbecue? Italian? Chinese?"

I shrug. "It all sounds good."

"Well, we can't go eat all of it, Lyzie," Cooper says, rolling his eyes. "I would surely be kicked out of my weight management group."

"Please."

"I'm only allowed one dinner per day, Lyzie. Just one dinner. One breakfast, one lunch, one dinner. You should see me at buffets. I'm just one of those sad men sitting in the corner with an empty plate."

I grin. "You're ridiculous. You are not in a weight management group."

He nods to me. "Actually, I am. I lead one with the firehouse."

"Seriously?"

"Seriously. It's part of our community outreach projects. We offer free nutrition classes, mostly for seniors."

I think about these poor seniors who have to come to these classes and sit there with an instructor who looks like Cooper.

That right there might send me into a different kind of support group.

Cooper has always been on the lean side but after college, he put on like fifty pounds of muscle when he was getting ready to try out for the fire station. He was insane about it. He would come over and ask Mike to go for a run with him and Cooper would be wearing two hundred pounds in a backpack that he would clip to his chest and waist while he ran.

The boy was insane.

When Cooper gets on a mission, he doesn't stop until he's successfully completed the mission. He's one of those people who would either make it to the top of Everest or die trying, but he wouldn't come back without doing one of those options.

It's one of the reasons that I don't like to mention things like climbing Everest around him. I need Cooper to not be taking risks beyond what he does every day at the fire station.

"You decide," I tell him.

"Mm. Barbecue. Have you ever eaten at Rex's? They're kind of newish. I can't remember if you were already in Carrington Springs when they opened."

I shake my head. "Never been there."

"Let's go there. It's really good. Little hole in the wall place." He nods toward the parking lot. "I assume you're staying the night, seeing as how it's already getting late for you to drive back?"

"It's barely six-fifteen."

"Yeah, but I don't like you driving after dark."

"Coop, I'm thirty-one years old."

"So?"

"So, this is the best my night vision is ever going to be, so you should just find something else to worry about."

He opens the passenger door of his truck. "Sorry. No can do. Before I take you for dinner, you have to pinky promise that you're spending the night at Mike's."

I roll my eyes and hold up my pinky. "I promise."

He shakes my pinky and nods for me to get into the truck.

"Good." He closes the door after me, goes around the front and climbs into the driver's seat.

"You guys worry way too much," I tell him.

"It's our job." Cooper grins at me. "So what's Mike up to tonight? Too busy to have dinner with his own sister?"

I shrug. "No idea."

He looks over at me sharply. "He doesn't know you're in town?"

"Not yet. I guess he will tonight though. Good thing I brought a change of clothes with me."

"Wait, so you came to see me first?" A different smile works around Cooper's mouth. "Wow. You came to me first? I don't know what to say. Apparently all these years of trying to pay me off to leave you alone were just jokes. I'm flattered."

"You should be."

"I'm either flattered or more worried. You okay?"

There's a nice, loaded question. Anyone else, I would have just nodded and said a chipper "yep!" so they would leave me alone and not press for more.

Cooper is a different story. You can't lie to someone who has known you since the day you were born.

"Um," I say, looking through the windshield and trying to figure out how to answer the question.

My phone rings right then and I manage a smile at Cooper.

"It's almost like you timed someone to call right then," Cooper says, grinning.

"Almost." It's not a number I recognize, so I don't answer it. But I do change the subject. "So this barbecue. Is it like ribs? Should I have packed a bib?"

"I see you trying to avoid the subject, but I'll let you get away with it. There's basically any kind of barbecue you can think of here. Ribs. Sandwiches. Wings. Everything I've ever tried has been great."

"Good to know."

"The real reason to go is for their sweet tea, though. It's seriously amazing. I have this feeling that they just pour it from one of those huge jugs you can get at the grocery store, but it's so good."

I grin. "Sounds good."

We get to the restaurant and Cooper parks right in front of the door.

"So the fact that there's only one other car here on a Friday night at dinner time means...?" I ask, unclicking my seatbelt hesitantly.

"It means the rest of St. Louis doesn't know what's good for them." He hops out of the car and we walk the six feet to the building.

There's a sign taped to the door.

CLOSED BY ORDER OF THE HEALTH DEPARTMENT

"What?" Cooper exclaims.

"Well, that explains the parking lot," I say.

"This isn't possible! I just ate here last week!"

"Gross. How's your stomach?"

"I mean, it was better than it is after I eat at Mr. Chow's."

"I don't think I want to know."

"It's good. Little hole in the wall place. We should go there instead."

"Is 'hole in the wall' Cooper Code for 'serves salmonella'?" I make a face. "Maybe we should stick to franchised restaurants."

"Mr. Chow's is good. And the perk of eating there is that the ensuing gastrointestinal distress makes all calories you consume kind of obsolete."

"New plan. I'm picking the restaurant."

"Kill joy."

"We're going to Olive Garden."

"Way to be like the boring, suburban American population," Cooper says, climbing back into the truck. "Don't you want to experiment?"

"Not with my intestines."

"Fair enough." He grins.

We drive to Olive Garden and the parking lot is packed. People are sitting on the benches out front, holding their buzzers and enjoying the spring evening. The weather is really beautiful in St. Louis this time of year. Few bugs, humidity is low, the temperature is in the low seventies. Come August, those will all be different stories and people will once again be cramming themselves into the waiting area of restaurants like sardines so they aren't melting outside.

"Two, please," Cooper says to the hostess after we squeeze our way to the front of the line.

"Two? Right this way."

I look at Cooper, who shrugs at me. "What about all the people waiting?" he asks.

"Oh, there's about six groups of eight or more here tonight," she says. "We have tables for two to spare. Right this way, please."

We follow her to a tiny booth tucked into the far back corner of the restaurant. "Your waiter will be right with you."

I sit down and open my menu, though I know I'm getting the soup, salad and breadsticks. I got the apricot chicken once and it was good, but by the time I ate the salad and breadsticks before they brought out the chicken, I was stuffed.

Better to just stick with the appetizers.

Plus, then I might have room for dessert.

"All right, Sell-out, what are you getting?" Cooper asks.

"Cooper, it's not selling out to try and not get food poisoning."

"That's half the fun in eating out! You never know what you are going to get!"

"Meaning listeria?"

He sighs. "You just have no sense of adventure, Eliza. But then again, you come from a long line of non-adventurers, so I guess I shouldn't expect differently. I remember your dad could barely handle it if your Mom changed her chocolate chip cookie recipe even a tiny bit."

I grin. "He did love his chocolate chip cookies."

"That he did. So did your grandfather."

I don't remember too much about my grandpa. He died right before Dad did from a heart attack.

The odds of me living past my mid-fifties aren't good, considering my parents and grandparents.

Nice, encouraging thought for the day.

"I'm getting the soup, salad and breadsticks."

"I'm getting the Tour of Italy."

"I figured." Some of this is probably due to Cooper's job and how active he is, but the man eats like a lumberjack. I've heard stories of steak eating championships at the firehouse and Cooper has like whooped everyone.

It sounds expensive. Food prices are so ridiculous these days. I can barely afford to eat some weeks and I make a really good living. I try to donate as much as I can to food banks because God help the single mamas who are barely holding on with this economy.

We tell our waiter the order, give him our menus and Cooper looks across the table at me. "So, why the secrecy today? How come Mike doesn't know you're here?"

I shrug. "I decided at like noon to come. Just figured I surprise him."

"But you decided to surprise me first?"

I play with my napkin. "I went to the gravesite today."

Cooper's face immediately softens. "Oh," he says and there is understanding in his tone. "I see." He reaches for my hand, stopping me from twisting my napkin around and around, lowering his voice. "Are you okay?"

This is something I both appreciate and don't appreciate about Cooper. He doesn't shy away from the hard conversations. Where some people change the subject or try to just smooth things over, he goes straight for it.

Sometimes, like right now, when I need to talk through my thoughts, it's nice. Sometimes, like often in the past, when I want to just process it and figure it out by myself, it's the most annoying trait on the planet.

I look at his hand on mine. His thumb lightly rubs over my knuckles and I feel like this should be weirder than it is.

It's kind of nice.

Cooper's hands have never been soft and smooth. He's spent too much of his life outside or working out or messing around with different construction things for that. And now that he's with the fire department, they're even worse. He's constantly bleeding from split

218

knuckles because his hands are always so dry and take such a beating. One time I bought him this hand lotion that was specifically for men because he always refused my vanilla-scented lotion, but I doubt he ever used it.

A teeny, tiny, gnat-sized sizzle runs up my arm and falls down into my stomach.

What is this? I almost yank my hand away but I don't want to be rude or weird. But this is *Cooper*.

I blink repeatedly and try to focus on something other than how warm his hand is and how gently he is holding mine.

I must be exhausted.

"Lyzie? Are you okay?" he asks again.

I take a deep breath and nod. "I'm okay."

"When was the last time you went?"

"Honestly, I don't remember." I feel guilty about this but Cooper is shaking his head.

"There's no shame in that question, Eliza," he says. "I was more just curious. They don't know, they aren't there. You could make pilgrimages there every night at five o'clock, have a picnic dinner there and toast them every single time. It still wouldn't prove that you loved them more. I guarantee that Jesus isn't up there telling them that Eliza hasn't visited their grave."

"You sure?"

"Positive. So, did you like the flowers?" He smiles all proudly, lightly squeezing my hand.

"You did them?"

"Sure did. I went with blue for Easter."

"Blue isn't an Easter color, Cooper. And why are you putting flowers up? Shouldn't Mike or I be doing that?"

He shrugs. "I don't mind."

"Cooper?"

"Yeah?"

"Does Mike go visit?"

He looks at me and I suddenly realize that Cooper's role in our family has been the Secret Keeper for both me and Mike, probably for the majority of his life. When I was younger, he was the one who was always around. Even if I didn't tell him things, he just instinctively knew.

It makes me wonder how much he's heard over the years, how much he knows that he's never shared.

"Mike doesn't go to the cemetery, does he?" I ask quietly.

"Very rarely," Cooper says, obviously trying to preserve my brother's trust.

I bite the inside of my cheek, feeling both thankful because at least it's not just me who has trouble there and also pained for my brother's sake because I know exactly how he feels. "Thank you for doing the flowers."

"You're welcome. And blue is an Easter color." He lightly squeezes my hand again and then let's go.

I'm not going to pay attention to the twinge in my chest that is disappointed over this.

"Coop. It's really not."

"What holiday color is it then?"

I shrug. "I don't know. Hanukkah?"

He laughs. "I'll go save those for Hanukkah then. So what are Easter colors?"

"Pink and green and yellow, I guess? Like the pastel versions of the colors? I don't really know."

"Did you see the vase with the little bunnies poking out of it?"

I nod. "Yeah."

"I thought about putting just a bunch of mud-colored eggs in the vase but then I figured it would probably smell bad after a little bit and no one would get the joke."

I start laughing. "That year was classic."

I still remember it so well. Mom had come home one day all excited because she'd found this package of Easter egg dye on clearance.

"How old were we?" I ask Cooper.

He rubs his cheek as he thinks, smirking. "I don't know. I think I was about ten or eleven? Somewhere in there? So you would have been like six or so?"

"That was hilarious. Poor Mom."

We had decided to dye the eggs while Mom was gone somewhere as a surprise when she got back.

There was a reason the package was on clearance. Every single dye was like this nasty greenish brown color. But we kept trying because we thought we were leaving the eggs in for too long and then for too short of time and we ended up dying like the entire flat of sixty eggs Mom had bought. And we forgot to cook the eggs first.

It was kind of a shock to Mom when she tried to at least salvage the eggs for egg salad sandwiches. We ended up eating scrambled eggs for what felt like years.

"Thanks for not putting eggs in the vase."

He grins. "No problem. So, what did you do there?"

"At the cemetery?"

He nods.

I sigh and right as I'm about to answer, the salad and breadsticks show up. "Freshly grated parmesan on the salad?" the waiter asks.

"Most definitely," Cooper says.

"Please," I nod.

He shreds a tiny mountain of parmesan on the salad before we tell him to stop. "Enjoy."

"Glad I'm not the only one who likes a little salad with my cheese," Cooper says, grinning. "Pass me your plate."

I hand it to him and he puts a large helping on it.

"So, you were saying?"

"I mean, it was weird," I say, unwrapping my silverware and trying to figure out how to explain it to Cooper.

"I know."

I take a bite of the lettuce and chew it, looking at Cooper. "How often do you go?" I ask after I swallow.

"To the cemetery?"

"Yeah."

He shrugs. "About once a month."

I can feel my mouth open in shock. "Once a *month*? Are you serious?"

He nods. "Sometimes more often. Sometimes less."

Maybe there was a reason we always used to joke that Cooper was the favorite child.

"Well...I mean, what do you do there?" I stutter.

"I change out the flowers, make sure the vase is still upright. I don't know. It's peaceful there. I usually just go by after I get off work. I do a lot of thinking there."

Cooper works twenty-four hour shifts starting and ending at seven in the morning. I imagine it would be peaceful that early in the morning at the cemetery.

"So, you just sit there and think?"

He smiles. "Pretty much. I think and pray. Sometimes I'll do my Bible study there."

"You don't think it's weird?"

"That I'm visiting your parents' graves? I mean, maybe a little. But seriously, they were like my second parents. Really, your mom was basically my mother in almost every way she could have been."

I know Cooper loved my parents like his own. And he's right – in every way that counted, my mother was more his mom than his biological one. Mom cooked for him every single night. Mom made sure he was wearing clean clothes and taking a healthy lunch to school. When Cooper got sick, it was my mom who took him to the doctor and it was my mom who bought him his first suit and helped him buy the corsage for his prom date.

So, it's a little strange but not that strange that he goes to visit their graves.

But that wasn't really what I meant.

"No, I mean, you don't think it's weird to just be sitting there by them?"

"Eliza, it's not like they are there. Their bodies are there, but nothing else. It's just a quiet place to think. And I don't know. I like feeling like part of the family still. They pretty much took me in when no one else did."

I nod. "Yeah, I guess so."

"Why? Was it that weird for you today?"

I'm struggling to find the words. "I don't know. Kind of. I just don't know how to act there. And I feel like I should talk to them or something and it's just weird because I know they aren't there. And then it's even worse because then I start thinking about all these things that I need to tell them and they aren't able to listen or give me advice or anything." I'm trying my best to choke back the tears because goodness knows that Olive Garden is not really the place to break down.

I feel like the other customers might complain.

Cooper smiles a sad, kind smile at me. "I know," he says.

And I know he does.

"Your soup, miss," the waiter says, suddenly appearing beside my chair. "And your Tour of Italy," he says, putting a plate overflowing with food in front of Cooper. He leaves and I look over at Cooper's plate.

"Good night. You won't need to eat for a week."

"This? This is nothing. You should have seen some of the eating competitions we did at the firehouse."

He grins at me and nods to the food. "Let me pray." He folds his hands in front of his plate. "Jesus, thank you for this food. Thank you for Eliza and the gift she is. Help her to know Your plan for her life and please just comfort her tonight, even though she did not order comfort food. We love you. Amen."

"Soup is comfort food," I say, smiling. "And thank you."

"You're welcome. And friend, I need to introduce you to mozzarella."

"We've met, thank you. I still like soup. And there's really not any comfort food as good as chocolate cake."

"Okay, I'll concede that one."

"Or chocolate chip cookies. Or maybe a milkshake."

He grins.

CHAPTER *Sixteen*

I still have the key to Mike's apartment. I find an empty spot in the parking lot out front and drag my suitcase out of the car. I lived here for a long time. Mike's lived here for even longer. The Wakemans have officially over stayed the amount of time you should ever conceivably stay in an apartment.

I know Mike stayed at first so that things would stay the same for me after Mom died. But now, I have no idea why he is still here.

"So, what's your plan?"

I turn around and Cooper is behind me. Cooper and I looked at the desserts at Olive Garden and decided that it would be more fun to just make dessert at Mike's apartment. He basically invited himself over and then took me to the grocery store to pick up ice cream, apples and a can of crescent rolls. We picked up my car at Cooper's apartment and then drove the three minutes to Mike's.

"I'm going to knock and if he doesn't answer, I'm going to just go on in."

Cooper takes my suitcase from me. "I hope he's not in the shower."

"If he is, he'll learn you should always close the bathroom door when someone has your house key."

Cooper laughs.

I walk up the stairs holding the grocery sack and knock on Mike's door. A minute later, he opens it, grinning widely. "Eliza!" he shouts and pulls me into a hug.

"Notice he's not excited to see me," Cooper says, setting my suitcase in the family room. "Even though I'm the one who carted that suitcase all the way up the stairs."

"It's got two days of clothes in it," I say, rolling my eyes. "I thought you had to be able to drag three hundred pound people out of burning buildings. You can't even bring a suitcase up the stairs?"

"Nice to see you, Coop."

"Thank you. That's all I wanted. Just a friendly, 'it's good to see you, friend who is like a brother to me'."

Mike grins at me. "What are you doing here?"

I shrug. "I had time."

"I'm glad you did. Have you eaten dinner?"

I nod. "Yeah, but I brought stuff to make dessert."

"A sure sign that Eliza is in town," Mike grins. "I never have dessert unless you're here."

"Well, you might change your mind after this one I'm about to make. It's amazing."

"What is it?"

Both of the boys follow me into the kitchen and I wash my hands, reaching for a cookie sheet. When I moved out, in theory we split a lot of the kitchen stuff in half, but honestly, I left a lot for Mike too and just bought new. I knew if I didn't leave it, he would never replace it and then he'd be that sad bachelor who didn't own any spoons and drinks his orange juice out of a flower vase.

I turn on the oven so it can start preheating. I find butter in the fridge and pull out a medium skillet, putting a couple of tablespoons of butter in the skillet and turning it on low while I start peeling and chopping the apples.

"What are you making?" Cooper asks. "Apple pie?"

"No, it's way too late for me to be making a pie. But I did see a recipe for apple pie that I want to try soon." Might need to try it out on Katie and Ashten so I know I'll have leftovers to keep picking on for awhile. When I make desserts for Mike and Cooper, there are never any leftovers. And apple pie is one of those desserts that I can convince myself is healthy enough for breakfast.

Apples? Fruit. Cinnamon? Anti-inflammatory. Crust?

Well, we don't think about the crust. But if I put ice cream on top, it's basically like putting a big dollop of calcium on there. I mean, at that point, I'm pretty much eating a multi-vitamin.

This is how my brain works first thing in the morning without caffeine.

It's probably for the best when it comes to my waistline that I'm usually fairly caffeinated.

I finish chopping the apples and I butter the cookie sheet. Then I pop open the crescent rolls and spread the dough in a big rectangle on the sheet.

I dump the apples into the skillet with the melted butter, turn the heat up a little bit and then add brown sugar and a little cinnamon.

Mike's apartment smells like a fall candle now.

Both the boys are drooling.

"Holy cow, Lyzie," Cooper says, dabbing his chin with his shirt collar. "Whatever you are making smells like heaven."

"Can you make this every time before I have someone come over?" Mike asks.

"Who do you have come over other than me?" Cooper asks.

"I don't know. I could have company."

"Dude, you wouldn't know the first thing to do with company."

"Sure, I do. I would leave out the good hand towel in the bathroom."

I stir the apple mixture and the oven dings that it's ready. "Mike, you only have one good towel?"

"I think it's yours, actually. It's purple, so I never use it."

"Well, at least I know what to get you for Christmas."

"Please don't get me towels for Christmas."

"He'd rather you get him company," Cooper grins. "Come on, Eliza. Don't you have a cute friend you could introduce him to? You're kind of failing in the good sister category right now."

I don't mention that I've already tried with Katie. Maybe there's hope with Ashten. "You can come to Carrington Springs and meet some more friends," I tell Mike. "There's a whole Bible study with lots of girls that meets at Katie's house right across the street."

A weird look appears briefly on both of their faces, but then it's gone before I have the chance to say anything. Maybe it's the insanely delicious smell.

I pour the bubbling apple mixture into the center of the dough and then I cut slits along the sides and do a fake braid with the dough strips over the warm apples.

It looks pretty.

Not that it matters. Mike and Cooper could care less about the aesthetics of something, especially food. When I graduated nursing school, I had heard about this restaurant in town that was known for its gourmet tapas, so I asked to go there for my celebration dinner. I barely had a chance to admire the way they arranged the plates before all the food was gone and we were out sixty dollars for like three tiny meals. I think we all ended up making quesadillas at home afterward because we were all still starving.

I guess I learned my lesson when it comes to gourmet food. It's just generally best to not eat at those types of places with men in their twenties.

Particularly two men.

I slide the dessert into the oven and set the timer for twelve minutes.

"Movie?" Mike suggests.

"Sure." Cooper and I both nod.

Mike goes into the living room to start looking through the movies he has and Cooper looks over at me. "Are you going to tell him about visiting your parents? Or dinner?" he asks in a low voice so Mike can't hear.

I shake my head. "He doesn't need to be worrying about these things." I point at Cooper with the spoon from the skillet. "And you need to not tell him either. Mike worries enough as it is. Got it?"

"Yes ma'am," Cooper nods. "You're right, he does worry about you."

"Too much," I say, under my breath. "It's stifling."

"I know."

I'm sure he does. Cooper has been around for a lot of my freak outs when Mike started getting too overbearing.

You can only take so much from your older brother trying to be both your mother and your father.

"All right," Mike says, coming back over into the tiny kitchen. "We've got *Men in Black* or *Independence Day*."

"Well, that's ironic," I say, more for Cooper's benefit.

He grins.

Mike looks at me. "Why? Because they are both Will Smith movies? I was thinking it was a good day for the Fresh Prince."

"Have you ever watched that show and had this weird feeling like this cannot possibly be the same man who was in that movie about the homeless guy who was looking for a job?" I look up from washing the skillet. "What was the name of that movie? *Good Will Hunting?*"

Cooper starts laughing. "You're funny. And no, that one was with Matt Damon. But that would have been a good title for it. It was *The Pursuit of Happyness*."

"That's right."

"So which one?" Mike asks.

"Mm. *Independence Day*," Cooper says. "I think Eliza has been hoping for that for a long time."

"I mean, it's a good movie but not that good," Mike says, going back into the living room.

I grin.

I finish washing the skillet and wiping down the counters right as the oven beeps, so I pull out the golden brown, amazing smelling dessert out of the oven and both the boys are instantly in the kitchen.

"Oh my gosh," Mike says, closing his eyes. "What is it?"

"I'm not really sure," I say. "I came up with the idea when I was really hungry for something sweet one day and all I had in the fridge was an apple and a can of crescent rolls. It's pretty good though. It's not a chocolate cake, but it's not too far off."

I dig the carton of vanilla ice cream out of the freezer and start slicing the apple dessert into thirds, stick it into three different bowls and top it with a big scoop of ice cream and a little shake of cinnamon.

I think Cooper and Mike both need bibs with how much they are drooling.

"Can you come home every Friday night?" Mike asks me, taking his bowl.

"Are you still anti-homemade-coffee?" I ask him.

"As in, do I still not make it?" He shakes his head. "I just pick one up on the way to work."

"Seriously?"

"You took the Keurig!"

"Mike, coffeemakers are cheap. You could have probably bought one six times over with how much you are paying for coffee every day."

234

"Probably, but then the little espresso shop I go to everyday would most likely go bankrupt."

"Mike, if you are single-handedly keeping an espresso shop alive, maybe you need to seriously consider how much coffee you are drinking."

"I like my routine," Mike says, shrugging.

"So basically, you don't have any coffee in the house?" I ask.

"Basically, yes."

"Bummer. Coffee would be perfect with this."

"Coffee is good with just about anything though," Cooper smiles at me.

"Very true."

We carry our desserts to the living room and Mike has the movie queued up on the TV. "It's really good to have you home, Eliza," Mike says.

"What about me?" Cooper asks. "Isn't it good to have me home?"

"It's great. It's the best," Mike says. He looks back over at me. "How long are you going to be able to stay?"

"I work on Monday."

"I'm working Monday too," Cooper says. "So, I'll probably have to leave Sunday."

Mike ignores Cooper. "So are you going to stay for the entire weekend?"

"That's the plan. I'll probably drive home Sunday afternoon."

"Yeah, that's around when I was thinking too."

Mike is smiling at me and still ignoring Cooper. He makes me crazy with how much he worries over me, but on the other hand, it is kind of nice to be worried over. And it's nice for someone to get so excited about my presence.

"Feeling the love over here, peeps. Feeling the love," Cooper says.

I laugh.

Mike starts the movie and we all dig into our desserts. The warm apple has made my ice cream half-melted, which is my favorite way to eat it on pies or desserts like this.

Young Will Smith is trying to save the world from the alien invasion and the next thing I know, Mike is gently shaking my shoulder. "Lyzie, go on to bed."

I open my eyes and the credits are rolling. Cooper is gone and it's pitch black outside and in the apartment. I stumble to my old room and collapse in the bed.

I'm back out before I can even really process what's happening.

I wake up about eight the next morning and brush my teeth before going out to the kitchen.

There's just something about brushing your teeth. I'm never really up for the day until I do it. I've heard of people who have to wash their face or take a shower or make their bed or something, but for me, it's brushing my teeth.

Mike's bedroom door is open but he's not in the apartment. I look through the fridge for breakfast stuff.

Seriously, what does he eat? The only thing he seems to have plenty of is mustard. There's like three different bottles in there, along with two eggs in a carton and a stick of unsalted butter.

Who needs three bottles of mustard? Does he have like hot dog raves here or something? We aren't allowed to have a grill here, so he would have to be baking the hot dogs in the oven or the microwave.

I can speak from experience that unless the hot dogs are wrapped in crescent rolls and baked, there is no good that comes from trying to prepare a hot dog without a grill.

The front door opens and Mike walks in, carrying a cardboard tray with two to-go coffee cups in it and a box from the local donut company down the street.

"Morning, Eliza," Mike says, smiling at me. "I decided to splurge and get apple fritters from Shelby's today."

"Wow." I close the fridge and join him at the table. "You willingly spent money on fritters after we just had dessert last night? What is happening to you?"

"Probably weight gain and early onset diabetes," he says, shaking his head and opening the box.

The smell is amazing. Shelby's is known for their apple fritters and specialty lattes. You know how some apple fritters are all cold and soggy and dense?

These are not like that. They fry them right as you order until they are crunchy on the outside and perfectly airy and soft on the inside and then they douse them in this vanilla icing.

I guarantee that Shelby will be cooking part of the feast in heaven someday. This is just practice for her.

"What kind of coffee did you get me?" I ask.

"I was recommended to get you the Milky Way since I was also ordering fritters. Apparently, it's the most popular combination."

I pop the lid off the top of it and inhale.

"Good choice. Thanks so much."

"Thanks. And you are welcome." Mike grabs paper plates from the kitchen and sits down to my left.

"What kind of coffee did you get?"

"Is that really a question?"

"So you went to a store that specializes in unique lattes and bought a black coffee?"

He sips it. "Their coffee is good too."

"It's just sad, Mike. And speaking of sad, what's the deal with the three bottles of mustard and no food in your fridge?"

He shrugs. "I don't know. Anytime I'm at the store in the dressing aisle, I always worry that I don't have mustard, so I pick up a bottle."

"You've only been to the store three times since I moved out?"

"No, but I've probably only been in the dressing aisle three times since you've moved out. Dressings tend to last me awhile."

"Where is all your food though?"

He shrugs again. "I need to go shopping. I'm running a little low."

"Yeah, just a little. You might have to have a stick of butter covered in mustard for lunch."

"I usually go out."

"For every meal?"

"Well, I mean, I usually eat eggs for breakfast and then I'm at work, so I'll go by and get a salad at that deli place by work and then I drive right past a little grocery store on my way home, so I just pick up one of those premade dinner tray things in the refrigerated section, like a fajita salad or something like that."

"Oh Mike. That's just sad."

"Well, my sister moved and left me to starve."

"You can cook," I say, rolling my eyes. "It's not like I cooked for you every night. I mean, you probably cooked for me more than I did for you!" Especially during school and when I was working.

"It's not very much fun to cook for yourself," Mike says.

I guess I can understand that. It does kind of ruin some of the joy of cooking if you are the only one who is eating it. I usually insist that Katie and Ashten come over whenever I'm cooking.

"Hey, so when did you decide to come up here?" Mike asks, switching gears in the conversation. He passes me a plate and I put a still-warm fritter on it. The icing sticks to my fingers and I go get a fork.

"Like noon yesterday," I tell him.

He looks at me for a long minute. "Are you doing okay, Lyzie?"

Mike knows me too well.

I nod, then I shrug and finally I just sigh. I take a bite of my apple fritter and chew it, looking out the window.

"Mike."

"Eliza."

"Do you ever…" I look over at him and try to figure out what I'm trying to say. "Do you ever think about Mom and Dad?"

"I mean, yeah. Like every day."

"What do you think about?"

"I don't know. What they might be doing if they were still here. What I might be doing. Sometimes I wonder what kind of advice they would give me in situations. Or I wonder how things would have been different if they had both lived. Would you have stayed in St. Louis? Would Dad have retired by now?" He sips his coffee. "Stuff like that. What about you?"

"A lot of the same stuff." I nod. "I've been thinking a lot about just the memories I have of them. Particularly Mom, I guess. She would have loved my job."

Mom loved all things that had to do with birth and babies.

She liked to tell me that if I had been a better baby, they would have never stopped. Apparently, my severe colic cured any desire they had for more children. In almost every one of my baby pictures, I'm screaming bloody murder.

So, I guess it's my fault that it's only me and Mike.

"I went to the cemetery," I tell Mike quietly. I'm not sure why I tell him. He's going to just worry more. But for whatever reason, I need him to know.

He looks up at me sharply. "Really?"

"Yeah. On my way up here yesterday."

"How, I mean..." He sighs. "So, are you okay?"

"I'm okay. It was weird. I haven't been there in a really long time."

"Me either."

I nod. "Cooper mentioned that he was the one who had redone the flowers."

Mike looks surprised to hear this. "Wait, Cooper keeps up the flowers?"

"Yeah. Who did you think did it?"

"I guess I didn't really think about the flowers. They're fake, right? Do they really need upkeep? I mean, isn't that the point of fake flowers?"

"Yeah, but they still get faded from the sun and stuff."

"That's nice of him."

I nod, taking another bite.

"Lyzie, can I ask you a question without you getting all defensive?"

I know what he's going to ask before he even asks it, but I can't answer him because my mouth is full. I guess he takes this as a yes.

"Why haven't you and Cooper just gotten married already?"

I almost gag on my fritter. "Mike," I gasp, guzzling some of my latte. I cough and choke and finally get my throat clear.

"What? It's a fair question. I don't need to tell you how great he is. And he has always had a thing for you."

I shake my head. "Mike."

"And I know what you're going to say," he says, holding up a hand. "And before you go telling me how it's just too weird, just think about it."

I don't need to think about it. "Mike, it would be so weird. We grew up together. It would be like marrying my cousin."

"It would not," Mike says, rolling his eyes. "Cooper is nothing like our cousin. We don't even have cousins."

Dad had one brother who was eight years younger than him and as far as I know, he's still living the single life in New York. We never really kept in contact with him. Dad always said that there were never two brothers who were more different than the two of them.

He came to Dad's funeral. He was there from the beginning of the service to the end of the service, he said hello and left and we never really heard from him again.

"So really," Mike is still talking. "Really, you have no idea what marrying your cousin would even be like, because we don't have any. And I've seen the way you look at him sometimes. And you guys dated, so obviously at some point in your life, you didn't find the concept too strange."

"That was so long ago," I say, waving a hand. "And it wasn't even dating. It was basically just what we do now except you weren't around. I mean, there was never really a spark or anything."

I will not think about dinner the other night and whatever it was that happened when Cooper held my hand.

I will not.

"It's the principal of it, Mike," I say, talking to myself as well. "We have known Cooper our entire lives. Like literally, there are pictures of him holding me the day I came home from the hospital. Don't you ever wish for things to be different? Or think it would be fun to have an adventure and see what else is out there?"

Mike shrugs. "Not really."

"Is that why you are still in this awful apartment?"

Mike looks around. "This apartment is nice."

"It's an apartment, though, Mike. You're thirty-five years old. Don't you ever want to own your own home?"

"I've looked a few times at buying over the years." He sips his coffee. "I've never found anything in St. Louis I liked enough to move for. Moving is hard."

"I know this."

"I know you do." He grins at me. "Still glad you left St. Louis and your overbearing older brother?"

"I didn't leave because of you," I say, because that's what you say. Even though, yeah, I kind of did.

He looks at me for a long minute and then sets his coffee down, folding his hands on the table in front of his fritter.

244

"Eliza," he says. "We need to have a little talk."

"I thought we were talking."

"Remember the last time I came to visit you?"

I nod, getting a little confused at what this has to do with anything. "Yes."

"So, it wasn't just a trip to visit you just for the fun of it. I had a job interview."

I think my brain is stuck. I swear I heard an audible *errt!* just as Mike said that.

Mike keeps going. "It was an interview with a start up company that's going to be based in Carrington Springs and needs an engineer. It's a great opportunity and I can really see the potential for this place to do really great. It's time for a change. I think you are right. I have lived in this apartment for too long. I really like Carrington Springs. It's a nice little town. And, obviously, it would be even better because I would be working like six minutes from your house."

Three things are just going through my brain on a continuous loop, like three little hamsters all running on the same wheel.

Mike is moving to Carrington Springs.

Mike is moving to Carrington Springs.

Mike is *moving* to Carrington Springs.

Okay, so maybe it's the same hamster thought and it's just running so fast that it seems like three.

"So," he says a few minutes of silence later, drawing the word out. "What are you thinking? You don't seem crazy excited."

"No, Mike, that's not it," I say quickly, trying to instill some joy into my voice. "I am excited!" Though, honestly, I'm not sure that's true.

Here's the thing. I love my brother. I am obviously pretty close to my brother and he's the only family I have left in the entire world. So, yes, it will be great having him closer.

The problem is that Mike is just such an older brother.

"Look, I know that I can be…" he squints out the window, thinking. "A little controlling," he says finally.

I smirk.

"Watch it. But, it's only because I love you and I want you to be safe."

"I know, Mike. But sometimes, it's okay to take a little risk every now and then. That's part of living a full life."

"Not true. It's part of potentially dying an early death."

I sigh. "Mike."

"Lyzie, I know. And I'm going to try my best to stay out of things and let you live your life. But honestly, I'm kind of excited about the possibility of the change. It's going to be good for me, I think."

I definitely think it's a good thing for Mike to move. He has been stuck in the same thing for way too long. Routine is good. Spinning your wheels is not.

"So, when do you move?" I ask.

"I start on the first on the month."

"That's this coming Tuesday. Do you even know where you're moving to?"

He nods. "I signed a lease at a short term apartment close to the hospital and my work. I've been looking at houses online but I haven't found anything that I'm super excited about yet."

"Wow."

"I know."

I look around the apartment and suddenly, even though I think this is a really good thing for Mike to do, I get really overwhelmed with memories of Mom here. Mom standing right there in the kitchen, making us French toast. Mom sitting in the rocking chair by the front windows when I would get home from school.

"Weird, isn't it?" Mike says quietly, obviously noticing what I'm thinking about.

I never really got sad when I moved from here to Carrington Springs. If anything, I felt like this huge weight of the past was lifted off my chest and I was finally able to breathe again. I could be whoever I wanted to be and do whatever I wanted to do.

6

But somehow, Mike moving makes it really official that we are saying goodbye to the memories we have in this little apartment.

"How come you didn't tell me all this before?" I ask.

"I don't know," he shrugs. "I know you need some independence. And trust me, I'm going to do my best to stay out of your business when we are living in the same town again. But I don't know. I didn't want to tell you over the phone."

"So, if I hadn't have come, would you have just shown up at my door?"

"Probably."

"Lame."

"I know."

"When does the moving truck come?"

"I'm renting it on the 30th. I have to be out of here by five o'clock that day."

I look around. "Don't you think you should maybe start packing?"

He grins. "And guess what my weekend plans included? And since you lived here for a long time too, guess who gets to now help?"

"Joy. I'm so glad I came back."

He laughs.

CHAPTER *Seventeen*

Six hours later, I am surrounded by all of my junior high and high school memories on the floor of my old room.

About ninety percent of this stuff was ridiculous for me to hang on to. I mean, I have about fifteen notebooks from science and math classes here.

Why I thought I would need my notes from Algebra, I have no idea.

Maybe I was worried that one day I would lose a letter x and not know how to find it.

"Mike!" I yell.

"Yeah?"

"I need another trash bag!"

Mike appears in the doorway, without a trash bag. "Lyzie, you don't have to throw everything away," he says.

"I don't want these things. Do you want them?"

"Not really, but I just don't like the idea of you throwing all your memories away. I mean, you held onto all of it for this long."

"Because it was lost in the back of my closet," I say. "Trust me, Mike. If I'd known that I'd mislabeled a few boxes, I would have thrown all this stuff away years ago."

"Okay, but I'm just saying that you don't need to feel like you have to get rid of everything. I mean, I am leasing a three bedroom apartment there. I can just keep everything in the third bedroom if you'd like me to."

Meet my brother, Mike the Packrat. For being as clean as he is, the man cannot let go of anything.

Last I heard, he still had the cast from his arm when he broke it in the second grade. I mean, the thing should probably be donated to science by this point.

But Mike still holds on to it. Hopefully it's in some kind of a plastic bag or something because yuck.

"So you're going to have the entire third bedroom be just boxes?"

"I have been researching how to make a couch out of them," Mike says, grinning at me.

"You're ridiculous."

"Thanks."

"Knock-knock!"

We both look up as we hear Cooper's voice from the living room.

"I thought you took away his key," I say, loud enough for Cooper to hear.

"Didn't anyone hear me?" Cooper sticks his head in the doorway. "I said 'knock-knock'. You're supposed to say, 'who's there?'"

"Who's there?" I ask, taking the bait and rolling my eyes.

"Interrupting cow."

Mike grins.

I sigh, close my eyes and finally just say it. "Interrupting cow wh—"

"MOOOO!" Cooper yells.

Mike starts laughing and I just shake my head, trying not to smile because it will just make him continue to tell jokes for the rest of the night.

You can only take about three of Cooper's jokes before your soul starts to slowly die and you lose all the will to live.

"So, I take it you told her?" Cooper asks Mike.

"Told me what?" I ask.

"He's moving to Carrington Springs."

"What?" I insert enough shock into my voice to bring a patient on *Grey's Anatomy* back from the dead.

Cooper looks sharply at Mike, who just sighs and shakes his head.

"Whoops," he says. "Sorry man."

"Good going, Coop."

"Where are you going to live?" I ask Mike, trying to insert some emotion into my tone.

"With you," Mike says, shrugging. "You have the room and I need a place to stay. It will be like old times, Lyzie!"

"What?"

Cooper is rubbing his face. "Okay, now, Eliza, it's going to be fine. He's just kidding, he's already leased an apartment."

"He told me."

"You're a terrible person." Cooper shakes his head. "Both of you are terrible people."

"Why do you think I'm sitting here reading my old Chemistry notes?" I ask Cooper.

"Because you are trying to figure out what it is between us?"

Mike chuckles. "Nice one."

"Heh. Right."

Cooper grins, his dimple appearing. The way he looks at me sometimes makes my stomach feel like it's getting pressed through one of those machines that makes the swirly frozen yogurt.

Probably it makes me nervous because I don't like the thought of constantly letting him down.

Or maybe my stomach is all weird because I had a sugary apple thing for dessert last night and I had a sugary apple thing for breakfast this morning. Maybe my tolerance for sugar is decreasing the older I get.

It's definitely not because of anything between me and Cooper.

Definitely not. That ship has sailed.

Cooper grins at me. "Can't blame a guy for trying."

"But you can blame him for not moving on with life."

"Never give up, never surrender," Cooper nods to me.

"Ah yes, your family motto that hails all the way back to when *Galaxy Quest* was released," I say.

Cooper sighs. "I have told you this a thousand times that my dad was saying it way before Tim Allen ever did."

"Mm-hmm."

Mike shakes his head at us. "Well, I'm back to packing up my room. Cooper, you want to take the study?"

"Not particularly."

"Boxes are in the laundry closet."

"Glad you finally found a good use for that space," Cooper says as Mike leaves.

I took the washer and dryer when I moved out because Mike insisted and swore up and down that he was wanting to get a new washer and dryer anyway. It was like two months later and I asked how he liked his new washer and dryer and he told me he still hadn't gotten around to getting them. And now it's been almost a year.

And he's still using the Laundromat downstairs.

Just ridiculous.

"I do not understand why he never bought a new washer and dryer," I say. "It's not like they are super expensive. I mean, you can get a perfect condition one off Craigslist for nothing."

Cooper shrugs at me. "He told me one time that he went to the Laundromat because it was a social event."

"That's just sad."

"Kind of my thought too. Which is why I kind of encouraged him to look into Radiator Springs."

"*Carrington* Springs."

"Right." Cooper grins and grabs my old desk chair, flipping it around and straddling it, folding his arms on the top.

"I thought you were assigned to pack the office."

"I just want to talk with you for a few minutes without Mike around. Is that so bad?"

"Depends on what you want to talk about, I guess," I say.

Cooper's brown eyes are soft and gentle as he looks at me.

The twinge in my stomach is back in full force.

I have got to go back home. This is getting ridiculous.

Cooper lowers his voice. "You okay with him moving there?"

I haven't had a lot of time to think about it, but so far, I'm doing better than I would have ever thought I would be doing. I shrug. "I guess so."

"I think it will be good for him."

"I just want to make sure that he doesn't start freaking out about everything again," I say. The distance has been good for the both of us. And I know that Mike knows he can be overbearing. Hopefully, he can keep the lid on his thoughts on most things.

I'm one of those people that if I want an opinion, I'll ask for it. Maybe it's the nurse coming out in me. You only are in nursing for so many minutes before you realize that if you don't just make the decision yourself, nothing is ever going to be decided. Any case I've had where multiple doctors had to be paged to come figure out what to do for someone just becomes this huge, long process. And once a doctor gives an opinion, it's a huge deal that the nurses follow it. So, I try my best to avoid getting opinions unless it's totally necessary.

Everyone is much happier when there aren't random opinions being expressed all the time.

Cooper nods and I know he gets it. "I think he'll be much better than he was. It's been good for him for you guys to have some distance. But I think it will be even better for him to have you close again. He's lonely, Eliza."

This makes my heart hurt.

"There isn't anyone?" I ask, even more quietly. I really don't want Mike to hear us talking about him and his loneliness.

Cooper shakes his head slowly, pressing his lips together.

"I mean, he has me," Cooper says. "And we all know that if you have me, you rarely need anyone else in your life."

"Because you're so overwhelming?" I ask, smirking.

"No," Cooper says, rolling his eyes. "I mean, I am only telling you this because we are such close friends," he says, tucking his head down, eyes all serious on mine. "And I really don't like to brag, but I've been told by many people that my personality is just so magnetic and larger than life, that I am enough person for like twelve people."

I can't help it. I laugh. Which is always a mistake, because then he keeps going.

"So, you know, I try to tone it down most of the time, just for other people's sake. I don't want to make people too uncomfortable."

"That's just so kind of you," I say, shaking my head. His eyes are all sparkling and crinkled up in the corners. Cooper has always had this really cute, squinchy smile.

"Thanks!"

I move more of my old notebooks from biology to the trash pile. "So, you're going to be here all by yourself then," I say, changing the subject.

"Worried about me, huh?" Cooper grins. "I knew you really did care about me."

I sigh and shove my stomach and all it's twingey-ness back down into my gut where it belongs. "Never mind."

He smiles at me, slaps the back of the chair and stands. "All right. Off to pack up the office, since that is apparently my room of this apartment."

"I'll bet you ten bucks that you find more to keep than I do."

"You're on."

CHAPTER *Seventeen*

I decide to spend my brand new ten dollars on an appetizer for the three of us to share at Chili's later that night.

"Thank you for your help, guys," Mike says, dipping a chip into the guacamole. "There's no way I could have packed up that apartment by myself."

"No, there really isn't," Cooper nods. "And by the way, I submitted an application on your behalf to *Hoarders*. You should be hearing back soon, I would imagine."

"Very funny. Don't forget the box of stuff we just put in the back seat of your truck."

Cooper grins.

"So, really, Cooper, what are you going to do when we are both gone?" I ask, reaching for another chip. I love Chili's chips. And they are bottomless, so I always take advantage of the system and keep ordering refills until I'm so stuffed full of chips that I could be sick. And then I just ask for a to-go bag for them.

Cooper shrugs. "Contrary to popular belief, I do know other friends."

"Name three," Mike says.

"Chandler, Monica and Joey."

"Three *actual* friends."

"They are actual friends. They are *the* Friends, when you think about it."

I crunch my guacamole-loaded chip. "Do you think that part of the problem with our generation is we grew up on *Friends* and that's what we think our adult life should be like now?"

"What do you mean?" Mike asks.

"I mean, we think we should just be sitting around drinking coffee and dating really attractive people. And instead, we have to work real jobs and pay the rent on time and buy toilet paper."

"And date unattractive people?" Cooper asks.

"Exactly."

Mike grins. "You might have a point, Eliza."

"So, I never heard any real friends' names," I say to Cooper. I am kind of worried about him. Mike and I have each other at least. Other than the two of us, though, Cooper really doesn't have anyone. His dad is still pretty much absent in his life. I know he's close with his firefighter coworkers, but that's about it.

He waves a hand. "You guys worry too much," he says. "And it's not like you're both going to be on the other side of the moon. People have daily commutes that are farther apart than St. Louis and Carrington Springs."

The idea of someone driving more than one and a half hours twice a day to and from work is just crazy to me. Maybe it's because I grew up in Missouri, but even going to the next town over was a big deal. Mom would plan for like a week and buy special car trip snacks and stuff.

I can't imagine growing up somewhere where an hour and a half drive was just considered a normal part of every day life.

Even now, when I come back to St. Louis, I stay at least a day, or in this case, three days.

Our food comes and the boys both got steaks, which is pretty typical. Every time I come to Chili's, I get the honey chipotle chicken crispy things and every time I leave Chili's, I regret getting the honey chipotle chicken things. They are so heavy and so greasy and they do not reheat well, but I can never finish the entire plate and I have this mental block on leaving food at the table. Maybe I got one too many "starving kids in China" lectures as a child, but I'll even take home leftovers of a meal I hated and force myself to eat it over the next few days.

So, tonight I broke tradition and ordered a salad.

It sounded good. I think it has mandarin oranges in it. Salads should always have some sort of a fruit or cheese other than cheddar in it.

I don't say these things to Cooper. He would immediately give me a salad with cut up bananas and torn pieces of American cheese on it.

Sorry, America. You pretty much completely missed the podium in the "cheese" category. I'm not sure you were even in the same building, much less the same competition.

The waiter sets my salad in front of me and it's gigantic. Both of the boys immediately lean over, eyebrows furrowed.

"Salad. It's called salad," I tell them.

"Why are you eating salad at a restaurant?" Cooper asks me.

"It's healthy," I tell them.

"Eliza, it's very important to me for you to know that you are perfect exactly the way that you are and your weight has nothing to do with the person that you are or are going to be," Mike says, eyes all serious.

"I have said it before and I'm sure I will say it many times again, I think you are beautiful," Cooper says to me.

My stomach is still acting all weird, especially right now.

I'm not going to think about it.

I just look at both of them. "I ordered the salad because I don't like the greasy feeling the honey chicken crisper things leave on my face, not because I think I'm gaining weight. Though, now I think I'm gaining weight. Do you guys think I'm gaining weight?"

"Not at all," Cooper says quickly.

"Definitely not," Mike says at the same time.

I'm not totally convinced. I haven't owned a scale in about three years, more because I took a personal stance against being tied to a number. If I feel comfortable with how my clothes fit, I don't worry that much about what I weigh.

I'm not even sure I know an accurate weight for myself. I haven't been to the doctor in at least two years.

Probably time for a check-up.

"But let's talk about salads," Mike says. "They only seem like a healthy option when you eat out. But really, they are hiding all kinds of calories and fats in the dressings and all the additives. Not to mention the high fructose corn syrup coating all of those little mandarin oranges."

"And the steak is...?" I ask, pointing to the huge slab of meat on both of their plates.

"Protein," they both say at the same time.

Mike and Cooper. Sometimes they are too much alike.

I get home Sunday around five o'clock and I look in the rearview mirror at Katie's house as I pull into my driveway.

Lights are on at Katie's, so I don't even go inside my house, but head straight across the street and lightly tap on the textured glass on the front door before trying the handle. It's unlocked, which means Ashten's home.

"Hello!" I call into the house.

"Kitchen!" Ashten yells back.

I walk through the living room and find Katie and Ashten in the kitchen. Ashten's wearing sweatpants and a Missouri State T-shirt, her makeup is all done from church but her hair is back in a messy bun. Ashten's hair is crazy curly. She's one of those people that I always envy.

But my major hair envy is of Katie's hair. It's long and naturally highlighted and like a mixture of straight and wavy, which means she can pretty much do any style she wants to have. She wants it to be curly? She just runs a curling iron through it. She wants it to be straight? She just blow dries it and then flat irons it.

It's kind of sickening to someone who has one default hairstyle.

Stick straight. I've tried every single "miracle" mousse or serum or gel on the market and almost every curling iron, wand or weird new device that looks more like a portable waffle maker. Nothing ever works. My hair stays curled for all of about six minutes before it just goes back to being straight again.

Katie is not-so-shockingly in her pajama pants and she's wearing a shirt declaring the merits of wearing a helmet while on a bicycle with a thin jacket open on top of it.

"Hey!" Katie grins at me and comes over to give me a hug. "Back from St. Louis?"

It's one of those questions that I never really know how to answer without my sarcasm level reaching an all time high.

"Well, duh," Ashten says for me and I smirk.

Trust Ashten to do it for me.

"So, how was your trip?" Katie asks, ignoring Ashten.

I let my breath out and sit on one of her bar stools. "That's a loaded question."

"Not loaded at all. Did you see Cooper?" Katie grins.

"Did you see Mike?" Ashten asks.

"Did he propose again?"

"Cooper, not Mike."

I smile and shake my head. "You guys are ridiculous."

Ashten sets three places at the table as Katie unplugs a crockpot and carries it over to the island, along with a long-handled ladle.

"It smells good," I say, trying to change the subject for a minute.

"It's a new creation. We will see what it tastes like. And I hear you changing the subject and I reject the change."

"Ditto," Ashten says. "Tell us about Mike and Cooper."

"After we pray," Katie says. "Ashten, pray for us, please."

"Jesus, we love You. We are thankful for You. We love Eliza and we know that You have a great plan for her life, starting with this amazing meal. We pray that you bless Katie as she prepared this food and we pray that you just give Eliza guidance and grace and truth. Amen."

I can feel tears pricking the back of my eyes but I blink them away quickly as Katie hands me a bowl and the ladle.

I rarely have people pray for me like that. At least out loud in front of me. I know that Mike prays for me, I just don't often hear it.

"Dig in," Katie says. "I'm getting the bread out." She opens the oven door, pulling an oven mitt on her hand and the rich, yeasty smell of freshly baked bread fills the entire room.

"Oh my goodness," I say.

Odds are good that I actually have gained weight with these meals I am constantly eating over here. Even when I make dinner at my house, I usually just make enough for everyone now and make sure they come over.

"You outdid yourself," Ashten smiles at Katie. "Looks amazing."

"Thanks. It's also a new creation."

"So, what is this?" I ask, opening the lid to the crockpot.

"Sweet potato and black bean chili," Katie says. "With chicken. And corn. And a couple of other things."

"Sounds good."

"And this is some sort of bread that has a touch of cinnamon and cocoa powder in it."

"Is it like a sweet bread?" Ashten asks, looking suspiciously at the loaf.

"It's not supposed to be."

"Interesting."

"Very," I say, spooning the soup into my bowl. "What made you decide to make this fall-themed meal in March?"

"Pinterest," Katie says.

I grin. "Ah."

"Yep. It's the inspiration of all things both good and evil. I saw a soup that was similar to this that someone pinned, but I didn't have all the ingredients and some of the ones I did have just sounded gross, so I changed a few things out. Here, put some cheese and sour cream on top."

"Well, it smells good," I say.

"You can't really make sweet potatoes smell bad," Katie says.

"I beg to disagree," Ashten says, shaking her head. "I think one of the worst smells on the earth is burning sweet potatoes."

We sit at the table with our bowls and the chili is amazing. Not that I'm necessarily surprised. Everything that Katie makes is delicious.

"So, start talking," Ashten says, looking at me. "How was the trip?"

"It was…" My voice trails off and I think about the trip.

How do I describe the trip? I started with visiting my parents' graves, then Cooper held my hand and it ended with helping Mike pack. Nothing about it was a normal trip to St. Louis.

"It was different," I say.

"How come?"

"So, I went to visit my parents," I tell them.

"Oh friend." Katie is quick to put her hand on mine that isn't holding my spoon. "Are you okay?"

I'm suddenly struck at how different my reaction is to Katie's hand versus Cooper's.

Something to think on later. Or never.

I nod, trying to change my mental direction. "I'm okay. I found out that Mike never goes to visit the graves. Which is kind of surprising. And so Cooper is the one putting the flowers on the headstone and keeping it looking nice."

"That's really nice of him," Ashten says.

"Yeah. And then, Mike told me he's moving here."

I say it all nonchalantly, but both of them pounce on that little tidbit of information like alligators snapping at poor defenseless baby birds stranded on the beach because their wings aren't all the way formed.

I need to go to bed.

"He's what?" Katie asks.

"He's moving here?" Ashten says.

"Why?"

"When?"

"Where is he living?"

"Not with you, right?"

"How do you feel about this?"

"Are you excited or are you dreading it?"

The questions come one on top of the other in rapid-fire, machine gun style. I'm calmly eating my incredible chili, waiting for the questions to at least slow down.

"Well?" Ashten demands, finally.

"He's moving here in less than a week," I tell them. "He starts the first of the month at some new little company. So I helped him do some packing."

"The first of the month?" Ashten asks. "This isn't some super elaborate April Fool's Day joke, is it?"

"I don't think so." But now that I'm thinking about it, I'm going to double check.

"Are you okay with it?" Katie asks.

"I think I'm okay." And I honestly think I am. Especially after talking with Cooper about Mike.

Hopefully, Mike will stick to it and not be the overbearing older brother again who could barely let me out of his sight without panicking. I know he did it out of love, but it just felt so claustrophobic.

"So, where is he going to live?" Ashten asks. "With you?"

"Oh, no. No, he rented an apartment."

"Good," Katie nods. "I think it would be really hard for you to live with each other again."

"I one hundred percent agree," I say. "The less he knows about my coming and going, the better."

"Well, you usually are just coming and going here and work, so he couldn't be that nervous over those two places," Ashten grins.

She's right.

Suddenly, I realize that all this time, I've complained and complained about living under Mike's thumb and not wanting to be predictable and wanting to go have an adventure and really, I haven't done anything.

I haven't even been on a plane since I was eleven years old.

And I can't blame Mike for that. I could have gone so many places by now, especially with my schedule. I could have visited New York and Boston and Los Angeles and all of the places on my travel bucket list.

Why haven't I done anything?

"Earth to Eliza!" Ashten says, tapping my shoulder.

I blink and look over at her, setting my spoon down and rubbing my face.

"What's wrong?" she asks me.

"Oh man," I say. "I haven't done anything!"

"I didn't accuse you of anything."

"I'm becoming exactly who I swore I would never be!" I'm feeling that rubber band around my lungs again and the inside of my legs is getting all itchy, down close to the bones.

I need to go somewhere or do *something*.

I'm going to turn into the person I never wanted to be. If I stay here long enough, I'm going to end up in the house I'm living in right now. And Katie will marry Luke and Ashten will find a house on this street and someone to marry as well and we will all have block parties and raise each others' kids and never leave this street.

It sounds like the American dream but I think I'm having an anxiety attack just thinking about it.

"Eliza?" Katie asks in a kind voice, reaching across the table and grabbing my hand. "Are you okay?"

"This is my chance to be who I want to be and go where I want to go and see what I want to see and I'm wasting it!"

Ashten looks at Katie. "Wasn't that a song? Like by U2 or something?"

Katie shakes her head at Ashten. "I don't think so. Maybe a country song? Or Taylor Swift?"

I rub my forehead. "Guys."

"Sorry." Ashten takes a bite of her chili. "So, what are you going to do about it?"

"What do you mean?"

"I mean, if this is your time to do what you want, then go do what you want to do." She shrugs. "What's something you've always wanted to do?"

I am having trouble coming up with things now. I grasp for something I can remember off my list. "New York," I say finally, saying the first thing I can think of. "I've always wanted to go to New York."

Katie grins. "I'm going there on Wednesday for a two day meeting. You should come with me."

Ashten nods. "Sounds like a great plan to me."

"Can you get off, Ashten?" Katie asks her. "We could all go! We could do a girls' trip to New York! I'll have to go to my meetings on

Thursday and Friday, but we could totally stay through Sunday evening and I'll show you guys around!"

Katie lived in New York for at least a couple of years. She lived in an apartment and took the subway and everything. The concept just sounds like a movie or a TV show or something.

Ashten is nodding, smiling, obviously excited. "I have always wanted to go to New York! I've got a bunch of vacation days saved up. I'll put in for a substitute teacher. Do you have the time off, Eliza?"

I think I'm supposed to work on Friday and Saturday, but I haven't taken any days off since I got the job, so I'm sure I have a little bit of time I could use.

My stomach is getting all tight and nervous just thinking about it.

It's one thing to wish you could travel and dream about traveling and complain about not being able to travel.

It's a totally different thing to actually plan a trip and do it.

Especially when it involves a plane ride.

My stomach is nauseous.

"Um, yeah," I say, trying to instill some excitement into my voice. "I can probably do it. Mike gets here on Tuesday. I need to check with the charge nurse at the hospital to see if I can have the days off." There's a little thought in my head like maybe she won't approve the time off and I can just stay home and not have to fly.

272

There's just something incredibly wrong about a metal tube of people being able to stay suspended in the air. I don't care how fast you are going, it just isn't right. It doesn't follow the normal laws of gravity.

I nod. "I'll check."

"Yay!" Ashten is grinning.

Katie is nodding, all excited. "Oh, this is going to be so fun!" she says. "I always dread these trips because business travel is just so boring and lonely. And I hate staying in hotel rooms by myself. I always get all creeped out. But this is going to be so fun! I already have a hotel room with two beds and a pull out couch, so I'll just add a few more nights on to it. And be sure to pack some warm clothes. There's supposed to be a cold front while we are there. But cold is way better than hot as far as walking around the city. Bring good walking shoes, because you will spend a ton of time walking, even if we take taxis and the subway."

"Can we go see some famous movie spots?" Ashten asks.

"Sure! Wait. Which ones?"

"Well, I mean, we have to go see where Tom Hanks and Meg Ryan fell in love at that park in *You've Got Mail*," Ashten says. "It's my favorite movie."

Katie rolls her eyes. "I have no idea why."

"Seriously? That's a great movie!"

"Which you've reminded me of every one of the four times you've watched it since you moved in. Can't you just close your eyes and see it on the back of your eyelids by this point?"

"Tom Hanks is so sweet in that movie."

"Eh," Katie shrugs. "I have honestly never seen the appeal."

"What?" Ashten asks, shocked. "Eliza, back me up here."

I smile, eating my soup. "Sorry, Ashten. I'm with Katie on this one. Don't get me wrong, I think he's a great actor. He's just not really my type when it comes to attractiveness."

"You people. I think it's almost like turning your back on your mother country to dislike Tom Hanks."

"Oh good grief," Katie says, rolling her eyes.

I laugh.

CHAPTER *Eighteen*

Tuesday, I am leaving work high on caffeine and with the approval to take a few days off.

Here's the thing. I love laughing and being loud and I think I do a pretty good job of convincing people that I'm a confident person. Maybe some of that is the nursing. I feel like I need to project this aura of confidence so people will trust that I know what I'm doing when I'm in the middle of removing a catheter.

But really, deep down, I am not a confident person at all. I think I have continual buyer's remorse for every single thing I do. Even something as dumb as using a different toothpaste than the hygienist recommends makes my stomach knot a little bit.

So something like a trip across the country when my last plane flight ended so terribly is making me a nervous wreck. I think my hands have been shaking off and on all day.

Maybe some of that is the six latte refills I got during the course of the day. Every chance I got, I was either sending myself or an LPN down for a refill.

Debbie, my charge nurse, was super encouraging about it too. "Oh my goodness, yes," she said, immediately going to the computer to block me out for the weekend. "You need a break, Eliza. I've been watching you lately. The spark is gone."

"It's not gone, it's just kind of dimmed."

"Where are you going?" she asked me.

"New York."

"Well, I can't think of a better place to relight the spark than the city that never sleeps," she smiled. "You have fun. And relax. And if you see Michael McConaughey filming a movie, I need you to squeeze his bicep for me."

I'd laughed but really, gross. I heard he doesn't wear deodorant.

But maybe that's just one of those ugly rumors started by a fan who wasn't feeling the love or something.

I climb in my car, lock the doors and text Ashten and Katie.

We are a go.

By the time I have my key in the ignition, both of them have texted back. Katie's text is just a bunch of confetti emojis. Ashten's text is in all capital letters.

YAY!

I drive home and my phone is buzzing constantly in my purse the entire five minute drive home. When I get to my driveway, I have fifteen text messages.

Mostly packing advice. And ideas for last minute Broadway musicals we might be able to get tickets to see. And Ashten pleading to go see the *You've Got Mail* set, some place from *How to Lose a Guy in 10 Days* and house they used on *The Cosby Show*.

Katie had written back, *What about Times Square and 5th Avenue and the Empire State Building?*

Ashten's reply buzzes right then. *Oh! Empire State Building is where Tom Hanks and Meg Ryan got together in* Sleepless in Seattle! *Definitely!*

I grin.

Apparently, we are going on a movie scene tour in New York.

I go in my house and call Mike. It's almost eight o'clock, I would imagine he's packing like crazy because he moves tomorrow.

"Hey Lyzie."

"Hi Mike. How's the packing coming?"

"Oh, I've been done for a while now. I'm just eating all my freezer food since I don't have a good way to transport it."

"Wait, what?"

"Yeah." I hear a ding in the background. "Hang on, the pizzas are done. Let me hand you over to Cooper."

"Well, hello, dear Liza."

I wince at the reference to the terrible children's song about a hole in a bucket. It's so repetitious and gets completely stuck in my head even just thinking about it. I can already hear the tune and I immediately start trying to think of another song so it doesn't start playing through my brain.

Too late.

"Seriously? Now it's stuck in my head."

Cooper laughs a maniacal, evil laugh. "Now you can remember me all the rest of the day. What's up? How's Mayberry Falls?"

"Carrington Springs. It's fine. I'm getting ready to skip town, though. So, you guys are doing what?"

"Eating. Mike said he was having a freezer cleansing party and I just don't like to let him party alone. It's just depressing for everyone."

"You're so selfless."

"Thank you for noticing. So, where are you going? On your way back here? You'll have to just visit me because I believe your brother is moving there. It's the word on the street, anyway."

"New York City."

"I'm sorry, we must have a bad connection. I thought you said 'New York City'."

"I did."

"Are you going to drive there?"

I can hear Mike in the background. "She's going where?"

"Hang on, I'm putting you on speaker phone. Mike's getting out the last pizza."

"How many pizzas did you guys make?"

The background noise changes and I can tell I'm on speaker.

"Five," Mike says.

"*Five?*"

Cooper is talking. "Yep. And we've got battered cod, three bags of mixed vegetables all steamed up, four hamburger patties and a gallon of milk. It's a feast for the only the refined of palate."

"Right," I say, rolling my eyes. "Sounds exactly like what they serve at the most gourmet of restaurants."

"Speaking of which, you're going where?" Mike asks.

"New York. Katie has a business trip there on Wednesday and so Ashten and I are going with her and staying until Sunday." My stomach is still all knotted up again.

"You're getting on a plane?" Mike asks and I can hear the incredulity in his voice.

"On purpose?" Cooper asks.

"Yes," I say, trying to instill some annoyance into my voice. Sometimes it's best for people to not know you so well.

"Wow."

"I'm impressed," Cooper says. "Good job, Lyzie. You've always wanted to go to New York."

"Yeah, I have."

"So it's just the three of you traveling together?" Mike asks and then I hear him hiss, "I'm just asking!" and I smile, because Cooper obviously either kicked him or elbowed him or something.

"Yes, it's just the three of us. But Katie travels there all the time by herself, so I'm sure we'll be fine. We're staying in a nice hotel and like I said, Katie knows her way around the city. She lived there for a long time too."

"Well, have fun," Mike says but I can hear the reluctance in his voice.

"I think it sounds great," Cooper says enthusiastically. "You've been a little down lately. I think a fun vacation is exactly what you need."

"You must have been talking to my charge nurse," I say. "She said exactly the same thing as you. Like same words and everything."

"She sounds like a very smart person."

I grin.

Wednesday morning, I am staring at the gangplank leading to the airplane, trying not to hyperventilate. You know in movies how the main character eats something or tastes something or smells something and they whoosh back to their childhood like they're in a vacuum? That's how I feel standing on the gangplank. I am suddenly

eleven years old and I can see the white faced people around me as I

lose my lunch in seat 12B.

Mike moved into his new apartment last night. His new place is

nice, if not kind of boring. It's so weird to see all of our old furniture in

the new apartment. Especially since most of it was Mom and Dad's.

He's maybe five minutes away from my house.

It's going to be weird.

Cooper helped him unload the U-Haul, gave me a big hug and

wished me luck on my trip. "Call if you need anything," he said. "I can

be there in four hours. But I know you'll enjoy this adventure. You've

talked about wanting to see New York since you were six years old. I

hope it's everything you think it's going to be." Then he'd given me

one more hug. "And text me when you get there so I know you

survived the plane. But it will be fine, Lyzie."

Now, reliving my eleven year old nightmare, I'm not so sure.

"Eliza? Are you coming?" Katie is ahead of me, looking the

frequent flyer with her business casual outfit and a suitcase that looks

like NASA created it. It makes my brown fabric suitcase that I think I

received as a gift for that flight when I was eleven look like it belongs

to a bag lady. I'm almost embarrassed to be seen with it.

I half considered buying a new suitcase but I couldn't find one I

liked that didn't make me nearly swallow my gum when I saw the price tag. I mean, seriously, who pays that much for what is basically a dressed up cardboard box to carry your stuff in?

Apparently Katie.

"I'm coming," I tell her, taking a deep breath and starting down the ramp.

I step onto the plane and my stomach feels like I ate at one of those Chinese food places like Cooper likes to go to. I pass row after row of people who all look at me and I swear they all know that the last flight I was on did not go well.

I sit down in the seat beside Katie and Ashten. Katie is next to the window and Ashten is in the middle, I have the aisle seat.

"Does one of you want the window seat?" Katie asks. "I've already seen New York from the air a few times."

"I'm okay," Ashten says. "Honestly, the window seat makes me a little claustrophobic."

I am focused on the seat back in front of me and making sure I am breathing in and out.

Ashten looks over at me. "You okay?" she asks.

"Yes. I. Am. Fine."

It doesn't appear that my staccato answer is a satisfying one.

"Really." Her response is not a question.

"Let's just say that the last flight I was on wasn't so fun for most of the plane," I say.

"Should we have provided ear plugs for the other passengers?" Katie grins. "Are you going to scream the whole time?"

"Is there one of those throw up bags in the back of the seat somewhere?" I ask.

They both laugh and then stop when they see that I am basically practicing my yoga breathing while hugging the back of the seat in front of me.

"Wait, are you serious?" Ashten asks. "I'll trade you seats, Katie."

"No, no. I mean, I wouldn't want you to get all claustrophobic. This is purely for your benefit here."

"Right. Thanks for being so unselfish," Ashten says, rolling her eyes and then handing me the bag. "If you throw up, I will disown you as my friend."

"Thanks."

"You don't need to be scared of flying," Katie tells me. "I do it all the time. You just have to look at it like two hours of mandatory sitting down and reading time. It's almost like a little mini-vacation."

"Sure," I say. I'm just sitting there, gripping the back of the seat with one hand and the bag with the other, repeating my mantra over and over again.

Deep breath in. Everything is okay. Deep breath out. Everything is okay. Jesus please keep me from throwing up. Deep breath in. We're all going to be okay. Deep breath out. We're all going to be okay. Jesus please keep me from getting sick.

I don't even really care that every person walking past me is staring at me like I'm a carrier for some awful bird or swine flu.

I feel a tap on my left shoulder by the aisle and it's a graying lady in the row across the way. She's giving me a pitying look and has a little pink tube in her open hand across the aisle.

"I get air sickness something terrible too," she says. "Take one and you'll be at least able to hold your stomach in. Take two and you won't even remember this flight."

So it sounds like I'll be taking two.

I read the label on the bottle and it sounds like just your normal over the counter motion sickness stuff and the pills match what the bottle says, so I take them regardless of my mother's voice in my head warning me against taking candy from strangers.

I don't think she ever told me not to take medicine from strangers.

Ashten and Katie are just staring at me with big eyes, obviously thinking that I have officially lost my mind.

Dear goodness, I might die.

"Thank you," I say in a hoarse voice, handing the pill bottle back to the lady.

"It's perfectly safe, don't worry," she says.

She seems nice.

I spend the rest of the flight praying. Mostly for me to continue to live, but miraculously, the medicine seems to calm my stomach and I even close my eyes for a few minutes. I feel a little better when I see the lady pull out a Christian fiction novel to read.

Lord, please just get me to New York.

The airplane lands a few hours later and I feel like busting out of the plane and kissing the floor, but I change my mind when I see the floors of the airport. Yuck. Maybe I'll wait until we find a clean floor.

We roll our suitcases through the airport and out into the muggy air. Immediately, the smell of exhaust and the blaring of horns meets us as soon as we pass through the double doors. Every inch of the sidewalks are covered in old gum stains and grease and who knows what.

It's not quite the romantic New York City that is depicted in the movies.

Looks like I won't be kissing this ground either.

Katie hails a cab and it smells like an old pair of shoes at the thrift store when we climb inside. The driver takes off like he's joining NASCAR. He makes a turn like he's planning on breaking into orbit and Ashten and I grip the door handles with white fists while Katie chatters away like nothing potentially life-threatening is happening right now.

"So, we're going to take this to our hotel and I think I need to run by the office but then we can go get dinner at Serendipity's and walk around a little bit. Tomorrow and Friday, I have meetings all day, so you guys are on your own during the day, but there's this great pizza place by Times Square that we need to go get dinner at while we're here." She keeps on talking, but right then the driver hangs a right that slams me into the door and I see the whites of another driver's eyes in the intersection as they barely miss colliding with my door and I'm back to praying almost more ferociously than I was praying before on the plane.

Since I didn't die in the plane, I will most likely die in this taxi. And I haven't seen the subway yet, but if the beginning of this trip is any indication, I could possibly die there too.

Wasn't there a movie about all these types of transportation?

I know that Jesus somehow picked us up and set us back down at the hotel because I honestly have no idea how we make it there alive and in one piece. Based on the whiteness of Ashten's face, I think she's thinking the same thing. Katie hands the taxi driver a wad of cash, which seems very generous considering the gambles he just took with our lives, and we climb out, grabbing out suitcases.

I don't even care what is on the street. I fall to my knees and at least thank Jesus and all the angels that I am here and not taking another ride in the back of a car in a body bag right now.

People are walking everywhere around me and not one person even looks in my direction. Apparently, this is common to fall out of a taxi and bless the ground.

This should say something about the quality of drivers in this city. Maybe that is why most people walk.

"Oh, don't be ridiculous, Eliza." Katie is shaking her head. "Come on, let's go up to the room. I need to run by the office."

I follow Ashten and Katie into the hotel and it's actually a very nice hotel. There's a Starbucks in the lobby and, unlike outside, it smells clean.

Katie gets our room keys and we take the elevator up to the seventh floor. She unlocks the door and slings her suitcase on the little end table in the sitting room section of the hotel room.

The room is nice. It's got a couch that supposedly pulls out into a bed in the front part of the room and then two double beds in the back part.

Katie's publishing house must shell out a pretty penny for this kind of square footage in New York City. I've watched those little videos about "How Far Does A Million Dollars Go" for housing across the country online.

New York never fares well.

I've seen backyard sheds in Carrington Springs with more square footage and probably nicer features than a million dollar house in Manhattan.

Katie grins at us. "And here we are. In New York! So my publishing house is just right around the block. I'm going to run there and do a few things and then I'll be back and we can go to dinner. I would suggest dressing in layers. It's muggy now, but the cold front is supposed to move in tonight."

Ashten nods. "Got it. Will we be driving in a taxi to Serendipity's?"

"No, it's just fifteen blocks."

The New Yorker is coming out in Katie.

"Just" fifteen blocks.

Heh.

I've seen people in Missouri drive down the street to get their mail and drive back up to their house. A fifteen block walk would be worthy of a medal for some of those people.

"Good. If we aren't getting into a taxi again, I'm taking a shower. My shirt has pit stains on it from the first ride."

"You two are ridiculous," Katie says, rolling her eyes. "I'll be back!"

She leaves and Ashten and I just look at each other.

"So, first impressions?" Ashten asks me.

I hate to say it because all my life, I've been taught that New York City is this beautiful, magical place where true loves meet on top of towers and people run through traffic jams to propose, but the city I just briefly saw out the window during the ride from some demented form of Disney World is not the same city I see in the movies.

"It's dirty," I say to Ashten.

"You can say that again."

"It smells bad."

"And the people are rude. If I hadn't have hip checked a guy, he would have just trampled right over you getting your suitcase situated on the sidewalk earlier." Ashten sighs. "Oh well. Maybe it was just a weird afternoon. Dinner will probably be better."

"Maybe."

"I'm going to take a shower."

"I'm getting in after you." I hope I didn't catch lice from that taxi.

I set my stuff on one of the beds and I check my phone as Ashten goes into the bathroom.

Get there okay? Did you survive the plane ride in one piece? How's New York? Let me know. I'm trying not to worry about you. It's a text from Cooper.

I'm not sure how to respond so I just let him know I'm here.

CHAPTER *Nineteen*

By the time Katie gets back from the office, both Ashten and I have showered and changed into nicer, cleaner clothes. I have on a simple dress that I was assured by several bloggers' reviews would be both fashionable and comfortable and could be dressed up and dressed down depending on the occasion and a light jacket.

I'm not sure how dressy people get to go to Serendipity's, but this is about as dressy as I can handle without wearing heels. And goodness knows I am not wearing heels to walk fifteen blocks.

Ashten is apparently in agreement with me, because she's wearing a skirt and ballet flats. She looks adorable, but Ashten rarely does not look adorable.

Actually, I'm not sure I've ever seen her looking anything other than cute.

"Ready?" Katie asks, grinning, coming into the apartment. "You guys look great!"

"Thanks," Ashten says. "This is my outfit that says, 'Hello. I'm ready to be an extra in a movie at the drop of a hat.'"

Katie laughs. "Oh, Ashten."

"You never know. I mean, I read that movie stars go to Serendipity's all the time. And they made that whole movie there. It's like a New York institution."

"True."

We take the elevator down and start the walk. People are everywhere, walking alone, walking in groups. Almost everyone is on their cell phones and those who aren't, are busy taking pictures. You can spot tourists six blocks away and I'm curious if I look like those people do.

It's probably the wide eyes and the permanent wrinkle in the forehead because of the smell of the city.

Seriously, these people need to invest in some outdoor air freshener.

There are constant honking cars, constant music from the stores we are passing, constant yells from the street vendors and cab drivers. The noise is overwhelming.

"This way," Katie says, nodding to the right and we turn down a less crowded street. "So, save room for frozen hot chocolate or a sundae," she says.

"You don't have to tell me twice," I nod. I checked Serendipity's menu as soon as Katie asked me if we wanted to go there and I already know exactly what I'm going to order.

I feel like you can't go wrong with pasta.

We get to the restaurant and it's this unassuming little shop off the street but there are people everywhere in front of it, standing around, sitting on benches, obviously waiting.

We could be here for awhile.

Katie walks straight in and tells them her name and they nod. "Right this way, miss."

Well. That's good news.

We are seated at a little corner table and handed menus and Ashten looks at Katie. "So. When did you get all big enough to bypass the lines?"

She grins. "Hey, I'm well known in this town. And I know enough to call ahead and make dinner reservations."

The waiter comes and we all order iced teas and our entrees. I'm getting some sort of tortellini. Katie orders a chicken dish and Ashten is getting a salad.

The waiter leaves, closing his notebook and Katie looks at me.

"So," she says, folding her hands on the table. "How's New York so far?"

"Different than I expected," I say, trying to be kind to Katie's old hometown.

"You don't have to be nice to me about it. Remember, I left here for Carrington Springs."

"It's kind of dirty," I say.

She grins. "That it is."

"And it doesn't smell good."

"I agree."

"And the people and places and cars are really loud," I say.

Katie nods. "Yes, they are."

"But I made it here without losing it on the plane." I'm not sure what was in those miracle pills that the lady gave me, but I remember the name of them and I am totally tracking some down in this city for the flight home.

"I'm very thankful for that," Katie says quickly.

"Me too," Ashten nods.

"Can I ask you a question?" Katie is looking at me and I nod. She looks up at the ceiling and the weird décor suspended up there, obviously searching for the words. "So, when you made this list and wanted to do all of these adventures, did you already know that you had pretty severe motion sickness?"

"Kind of," I say.

"And you talk about wanting to see more and do more, but I'm just curious, why did you move to Carrington Springs, which is an hour and a half away from home, if you could have gone anywhere with your job? I mean, don't get me wrong, I love that you live there and that we met and I honestly can't imagine my life without you now, but why Carrington Springs? I mean, it's not really bustling with adventure."

I think through the events that let to me moving to Carrington Springs. Mike and I were butting heads, Cooper had basically proposed again and I was so tired of everything being the same. I saw the job posting and it seemed like a quick fix and it didn't involve a plane trip for the interview.

I shake my head. "I don't know. I was originally looking in the Dallas area, but nothing ever came up like I was looking for."

I remember the night I found the posting. I had just come home from my job in St. Louis. Cooper was waiting on the apartment steps and he was all smiley and sweet and then said something about, "maybe someday if we get married" and I just freaked out. I walked straight upstairs and went right to the job listings site for nurses that I checked every single day and a job in Carrington Springs had just been posted like an hour before.

So, I called them the next morning, did the interview the next week and moved three weeks later.

It's one of the few impulsive things I've done I've never regretted. I love Carrington Springs now.

I'm curious if Mike will love it as well.

"I'm not exactly sure," I tell Katie. "I just saw the ad and liked the job. And the town is cute. And I felt like it was still close enough to home for me to still have some contact with Mike."

"So, how are you doing with Mike moving to Carrington Springs?" Ashten asks.

"Okay," I nod. "I'm not sure what it's going to look like with him there." I'm not sure what Cooper's life will look like either. He is just about as alone as we are. Really, it's been the three of us for so long that I have a hard time imagining him without me and Mike there.

But I don't tell Katie and Ashten that.

"Eliza, can I ask again about Cooper?"

I just shake my head at Ashten's question. "You guys worry too much about me and Cooper," I tell her.

"I'm not worried. I'm just curious. You keep insisting that there is nothing between you guys, but seems like you are always hanging out with him. He's in almost every story that you tell of your childhood. And you've mentioned that you dated him a long time ago."

I take a deep breath. I guess it's time to talk about Cooper with Katie and Ashten.

Goodness knows I've been putting it off long enough.

Plus there's something about not being in the same general vicinity of him that somehow makes it easier to talk about him.

"You guys want to hear the story?"

"Please," Ashten says, over-emphasizing the word.

"Yes!" Katie says.

I take a deep breath. "So I first met Cooper the same day I met Mike, which was when I was one day old and ten minutes after my mom got out of the hospital with me. Cooper's family lived across the street and he and Mike were best friends and played together all the time."

"Aw," Ashten says. "That's so cute."

"So, we basically grew up together. Cooper's mom skipped out on them when he was in kindergarten, so ever since then, he basically lived with us since his dad worked so much."

"When did you guys start dating?" Katie asks me.

"When I was in college. Only for about four or so months. No time, really. And it was just weird. Like, it didn't feel like we were dating. He never really held my hand or did anything out of the ordinary. He would take me out to dinner, but it just sort of felt like Mike should be there too. I'm not even sure if we actually had a conversation about breaking up as much as we just kind of fizzled out."

I think about those days and how I was convinced that it was obviously not right or I would feel a little more.

"So what are things like now?" Ashten asks.

I sigh. "I don't know. They are just the same as they were ten years ago. He's just a really, really good friend. He's family. He knows things about me and my past that other people will never know. Some of it is big. Most of it is small. He's been there for every major event in my life. But..."

Katie is nodding. "But?"

"It's just weird," I say again. "There's not really any spark between us."

I'm choosing to forget that night when he held my hand. I'm sure I was imagining things. Too much going on and not enough sleep likely led to a lot of that.

"So, has he dated anyone since you guys broke up?"

I'm not actually sure. I know he went on a few dates here and there, but I don't think anything has stuck.

"I think he's gone out a few times," I tell them. "I don't think anything came of it. Which just speaks to the level of girls he's dated. They must not have been too bright to let him go. Cooper is about as good as it gets. I mean, he loves Jesus, he's super kind and thoughtful, he has an actual job."

Katie looks at Ashten and then at me. "So you let him go because why again?"

"Yeah, I mean, I think you just basically called yourself a dumb person," Ashten says.

298

"That's different," I protest.

"Okay. How?" Katie asks. "Let's maybe review the facts. Cooper is cute, Cooper loves Jesus, Cooper is kind and Cooper has a job. So, the problem is...?"

"The problem is that I grew up with Cooper," I tell them. "There's no chemistry."

I think about his hand holding mine or the way his brown eyes sparkle and soften when he looks at me.

There's no spark.

Right?

Later that night, I pull the covers up to my neck in the darkness. Ashten and Katie were both out like lights the second they went to bed, but I'm having trouble falling asleep. The city is so loud still, even now and it's past midnight. I can hear car horns and people talking and music through the window glass and I've even got a sound machine app playing white noise on my phone.

I could never live in this much constant noise.

I click open my phone and load up the Bible app, turning to James. I've been reading through it faster than the study and I'm on chapter four. I read it once through in my regular translation and then again in the Message.

And now I have a word for you who brashly announce, "Today—at the latest, tomorrow—we're off to such and such a city for the year. We're going to start a business and make a lot of money." You don't know the first thing about tomorrow. You're nothing but a wisp of fog, catching a brief bit of sun before disappearing. Instead, make it a habit to say, "If the Master wills it and we're still alive, we'll do this or that."

I think, for Mom, this verse more than any other became true for her after Dad died. She never used to say things like that, but after he died, she would always say, "Lord willing" before or after any plans she made. Someone asked her to coffee? She would say, "I'll be there at eight, Lord willing."

At first, I thought it was weird but now, I can see why she did it.

We are just a vapor. Just a "wisp of fog", like this translation says. My parents and grandparents prove that. Their lives were here and now they are gone and someday, Mike and I will be gone and no one will remember any of their names or ours.

It's a sobering thought.

So what do we do then, Jesus?

If we are just here today and gone the next, I don't want to waste this life. I don't want to realize that I haven't lived. Maybe that's why I am so anxious for adventure. I see Mom and Dad's short lives and I don't want to regret not doing something before there's no time left to do it.

There's an icon next to my text messages showing I missed one and I click over to it right before I go to sleep.

Sweet dreams, Lyzie. I hope you are having a great time.

It's from Cooper.

I close my eyes and listen to the sounds of the city.

I know what I need to do when I get home.

The next day, Katie leaves at eight o'clock. "Here's some maps," she says, tossing them onto the coffee table as Ashten and I stand there sleepily. My hair is a tangled mess and Ashten can't stop yawning. Katie, meanwhile, is all dressed up in a gray skirt, blazer and heels. The only color she has on is her red purse. Her blonde hair is waving down her back and her makeup is perfect.

She looks like a Gap ad.

"I've traced out a few different routes for you. Call me if you get lost. Or find a cop or something. Don't go to the areas I marked with a red pen. And if you get lost, just follow the signs back to the subway and you can pretty much find your way back to here from wherever you are. And have fun. And don't eat from a food truck or a hot dog cart unless there's a line."

"We'll be fine," Ashten says.

"Watch out for people on bikes, they ride on the sidewalk half the time. And there's always construction somewhere, so be aware of people and hard hat only areas. And don't forget to bring a room key."

"We'll be fine," I tell her.

"I wouldn't keep more than twenty dollars on each of you in cash and make sure that you have your wallets in some sort of a cross-body purse because the pick-pocketers like to be in the tourist attractions."

"Katie?"

She finally stops talking and looks at us. "What?"

"We'll be fine," Ashten and I say together.

"Okay. I just want you guys to be safe."

"Have a good meeting," Ashten says, half-shoving her out the door. "Don't worry about us."

"Oh! And don't forget to—"

Ashten closes the door on Katie's sentence and looks at me. "She was never going to stop."

"Agreed."

We look at the maps on the coffee table and Ashten opens one. "Good night, she wrote us a legend to help us follow the path," she says.

"Holy cow."

"When did she have time for this?" Ashten asks.

Katie is sleeping on the pull out bed, so maybe she did it last night after Ashten and I both went in the bedroom, though I could have sworn she was asleep before I started reading my devotional.

We both thumb through the maps and I'm so overwhelmed by the time we set them down that I kind of feel like just ordering room service and staying in the hotel.

"So, how about we do this a little differently," Ashten says. "What's something we want to go see?"

I shrug. "Empire State Building?"

She pulls out her phone and types it into the GPS. "Should take us twenty minutes to walk there," she says. "I'll get my clothes changed. Goodness knows I'm not showering until I'm going to be getting into my clean bed."

I laugh.

We change and put on makeup and we are walking out of our hotel room about thirty minutes later. I'm starving.

"Want to stop by Starbucks?" Ashten asks me in the elevator.

"We're in New York, Ashten. Aren't there like little bakeries and coffee shops on every street corner?"

"I think that's Seattle."

"I thought it was New York."

She shrugs. "Let's go see. I'm sure we can find another Starbucks, if nothing else."

We walk out onto the loud street and there's a little bakery just a few shops down. It has a huge glass window displaying all the different scones and muffins and cinnamon rolls inside and Ashten and I both walk inside without even checking with each other.

It smells like a yeasted, cinnamon-covered heaven in here.

"Holy cow," Ashten says, eyes wide as she stares at the gigantic cinnamon rolls. "What are you going to get?"

"I don't know." The cinnamon rolls look incredible but the giant blueberry muffins topped with buttery crumb topping also look amazing.

Or the orange cranberry scones with Turbinado sugar crystals on top.

I have no idea. And I look up and see an entire menu purely devoted just to lattes.

I wish we had this place in Carrington Springs. This almost makes up for the death-defying cab ride.

"What are you getting?" I ask Ashten.

"Cinnamon roll. No, the strawberries and cream muffin. And a caramel latte. No, the cinnamon latte. Oh my goodness, I don't even know."

We step out of the line because we are obviously holding up the impatient business people behind us.

"I'm just going to get one of each," I say finally. "We can keep what we don't eat for dessert tonight."

"Done."

We get back in line and when we leave, we are holding a bag with a cinnamon roll, a blueberry muffin, a strawberries and cream muffin, an orange cranberry scone and a chocolate-filled croissant. And we are each carrying a latte. Ashten went with the cinnamon, I went with the mocha.

We are about forty bucks lighter than we were, but I have a feeling it will be worth it.

"All right, Empire State Building is that way," Ashten says, looking at her phone. We are eating our muffins as we walk, I've got the bag tucked in my purse. Thankfully, I thought ahead and packed my larger purse for this trip.

We walk and look at the buildings, the taxi cabs, the people. New Yorkers are a different breed of human. I think I see maybe two who aren't attached to their phone. And it amazes me that all these women are walking this city in heels.

I heard at least six different languages in the short walk to the Empire State Building.

Such a diverse city.

We pay our entrance fee and we're standing at the top of the iconic tower a few minutes later, looking at the breathtaking view of the city.

"Wow," Ashten says.

"You can say that again."

"I can't believe how many people are crammed into such a tiny area."

I grin, because I was just thinking the same thing. "It's pretty crazy, huh? It kind of makes me want to tell them about the wide open pastures in Carrington Springs."

"Don't tell them. We want to keep those pastures wide open."

I laugh.

We find a little coffee shop next and I stir my iced coffee with my straw as we walk out the door to keep touring the city.

"So, Eliza."

"So. Ashten," I say, mimicking her tone.

"Let's talk about you and Cooper."

"Oh for goodness' sake."

"No, I'm serious," Ashten says. "I just want to ask you a question, because I've noticed this about you. And I've been thinking a lot about it and praying about a good time to bring it up."

I'm immediately bracing myself.

"So, I've never actually met Mike, I don't think. But I've heard you talking about him. And I think he probably is a worrying type of person anyway, but based on the way he clung to you after your parents died, I think he coped by trying to have more control. By trying to keep those he loves close so nothing could happen to them."

I'm not sure what this has to do with me and Cooper, but I nod. "That's exactly what happened."

"You, though, reacted the opposite way."

I look over at her. "What do you mean?"

"I mean, I think you distanced people. And even now, I've noticed that when Katie or I get too close, you react by backing away or cracking a joke or changing the subject so you can keep some space between your heart and the world."

It's like someone has stretched a couple of rubber bands over my ribcage. My chest immediately hurts from the pressure.

I don't say anything because she's right.

"So, I just wonder if that's what happened with Cooper. You dated for what? Four months? Just long enough to start realizing that he was getting too close. I think that you are scared to love because you think they will be taken away like your parents were. And I think that you needed to get away from Mike because the more he held on to you, the farther you needed to be from him."

Ashten is too perceptive.

I sip my coffee, thankful for my sunglasses to hide the tears pooling in there.

"Anyway. Just some thoughts," she says quietly. She reaches over and squeezes my shoulder. "I love you, Eliza. You aren't going to be able to push me and Katie away. I just need you to hear that."

I nod but there's no way I can answer her right now.

We spend the day walking around, trying different restaurants and I buy a pair of knock-off Ray Bans sunglasses. By the time Katie meets us in front of our hotel, we are both sunburnt, tired and stuffed to the brim, but Katie wants to show us Times Square and eat at a pizza place there, so we bandage our blistering feet and start off again.

This city is something else.

CHAPTER *Twenty*

Tuesday morning and I am back at work, yawning.

We didn't even get back to our street until after midnight on Sunday and I spent all day yesterday catching up on laundry and grocery shopping. Mike is supposed to come for a late dinner tonight after I get off work.

"How was New York?" Debbie asks, passing me in the hallway.

"Good," I nod. "Busy. Loud. Expensive."

She nods. "Sounds about right."

"Food was delicious, though. And we got to see *Wicked* on Broadway."

"Oh my goodness." Debbie clasps her hands to her heart. "I have always, always wanted to see that! Was it amazing?"

"It was." I can't really do it justice.

"I have friends who go to New York twice a year and they always talk about potentially living there someday. Would you want to do that?"

I don't have to think very long about that. "No, definitely not. It's not clean and it's just too loud." I think I've gotten used to the small town life.

Debbie nods. "Good. I wouldn't want to either. Plus, in order to live somewhere halfway decent, you have to either inherit something or be loaded beyond anything you could ever imagine."

"Exactly."

"Well. I'm glad you had a good time."

"Thanks. Thanks for the days off too."

She waves a hand. "Don't mention it. Did you get your schedule for this week?"

I nod. I'm off tomorrow, but then I work Thursday, Friday and Saturday. All day shifts, though, so it's not too bad.

I get home that night about seven-forty-five and as soon as I pull into the driveway, I can smell something.

Hopefully it's Mike or Ashten cooking and not my bedroom that's on fire.

I open the door and Mike greets me in the kitchen. "Hey there, Eliza."

"Used the spare key, I see," I say.

"Yep. So, your oven is a little weird, but I got it figured out and our lasagna should be done in about ten minutes. I was hoping it would be done by the time you got home."

He's got a big salad in a bowl, too. And a tray of watermelon. Which, sad to say, does not look fantastic but it's not watermelon season, so I guess I can't expect too much.

"Wow, if this is the kind of feast I can expect to come back to every day, then I'm really glad you moved here," I say, grinning, sitting at the counter on one of the bar stools.

"It's my welcome home to me and you feast," Mike says, handing me a plate. "You can at least get started with your salad."

"Thanks."

We talk about New York and I tell him about some of the things I saw. "My favorite place wasn't a tourist spot at all," I tell him. "It was just this little hole in the wall bakery that Ashten and I discovered the first morning there and then we just ate there every morning after that. Best cinnamon rolls and muffins I have ever had in my entire life."

"Sounds amazing."

"It was so good. I'm so thankful that we don't have one here, though. I wouldn't be able to fit into my pants."

Mike grins.

"How's the new job?" I ask.

He nods. "It's good. You know, it's really good. I think I'm going to really enjoy this new job. It's small and the place really feels like a career I can enjoy instead of just another cog in the wheel."

"That's great, Mike."

"So, what are your plans for this week?" Mike asks me, pulling the lasagna out of the oven.

"I'm off tomorrow," I say and then I try to quickly move on, because even though I'm off, I have plans. "Then I'm working the next three days. You?"

"Work."

"I figured."

"Can I come with you to church on Sunday?"

I nod. "Sure. I think you'll like it. And tomorrow night, there's a Bible study that meets at Katie and Ashten's house. You should come."

"Yeah, we'll see. Thanks Eliza."

The next morning, I am up and backing out of my driveway by seven in the morning. Which is not my favorite hour at all on my day off.

But I have things I need to do.

I glance over to the passenger seat and check for the sixtieth time that the basket I had packed earlier is still there. And it is.

The drive takes me longer than normal due to the extra morning traffic. I cannot imagine driving this every day, but apparently, quite a few people do.

I get to the cemetery at almost nine. A little later than I had hoped for, but I'm here and that's what matters. I park along the street, gather my wallet, keys and basket and walk over to the shade trees by Mom and Dad's graves.

It's cool and quiet here. There's mist on the grass and the trees and I'm not sure if it's dew or sprinkler remnants, but I'm glad I have a blanket in the basket.

I look at the headstone for a few minutes, trying to get up the nerve.

"Well, I'm here," I say quietly.

I set the basket down, pull out the blanket and spread it out beside the headstone, under the shade. I sit down and crisscross-applesauce my legs, like my Kindergarten teacher would always say in a sing-song voice. Then I take a deep breath, biting the inside of my bottom lip and reach back inside the basket.

I pull out the envelope and hold it with both hands, looking at my name in my mother's handwriting across the front of it.

Eliza.

Mom had always told me how much she loved my name. "You were named for your grandmother and for Elisabeth Elliot, the missionary," she would tell me. "A woman who loves Jesus greatly."

I take another deep breath and I can't help the nerves starting deep in my stomach.

It was only fitting that I read this letter here.

I turn it over and slide my thumb under the corner seal. The light blue paper is folded neatly inside and I pull it out, my hands shaking.

I look at the paper for a long time before opening the folds and turning it to the first page.

Sweet Eliza.

I lose it at my mom's handwriting. Tears are pooling in my eyes and spilling down my face and I hold the papers out so they don't get tear spots on them.

I pull in a jagged breath, wipe my eyes and keep going.

Sweet Eliza,

You, my dear girl, are the daughter of my heart. Which means that I know it has been many years since I have gone to be with Jesus and your dad by the time you are reading this letter.

I shake my head, managing a smile.

You are so loved, my sweet Eliza Lorraine. Your dad insisted I name you after me, by the way. He told me as soon as we heard the doctor telling us that you were a girl. Dad looked over at you and said you looked just like me and that no matter what, your name needed to have Lorraine in it somewhere. "This way, you'll always be with her," Dad told me.

I had no way of knowing then what I know now. This life will not be not easy for you, Eliza. God grants some people roads that are smooth and unencumbered. And God grants others roads that are uphill and full of rocks and briars. I always wanted to pray an easy path for you, precious daughter, but from the beginning, I knew in my heart that it was not the prayer you needed. So I prayed for grace. I prayed for laughter. And I prayed for dear friends who would come alongside you and walk with you and occasionally, if needed, carry you down this path and help you to know that you are not alone.

You are not alone, Eliza. You will never be alone. You are blessed with a brother who has loved you from the moment he first felt you moving within my womb. And you are blessed with a friend who will be here for you no matter what happens. Michael and Cooper are gifts and ones I hope you have learned to treasure, despite the annoyance they can cause you.

Eliza, right before your dad's accident, we were talking about you and Michael, as we often did late at night before we went to sleep. And we started praying for you both, as we did every night. And every night, we prayed for three things for you. We prayed for you to be full of grace. We prayed for you to be full of joy. And we prayed for you to someday find the same love that your dad and I found. And I know that I am not around and that it has been many years but I will tell you a secret fourth prayer that I always added onto my prayers for you: I prayed for you to find love with one who has loved you with all his heart since he was a four year-old.

Eliza, you have always craved that which was just out of your reach. But oh, my darling, do not make the mistake of tossing aside the diamond, be it rough, in your hand for the rhinestone on the shelf. Though one shines brightly now, it will not hold up under the pressure that life will put you through. And love will bring loss, but you must not trade the memories to be made for the safety of a life without knowing love.

I love you. I can't put into words how much I love you. You are the daughter of my heart, the joy of my life. I could never hope for anything more than you. May God bless you, my love, and keep you. May His face shine on you and give you peace.

Mom

I can't see the page anymore from the tears. I am gasping for breath, swiping at my wet cheeks, backhanding my running nose.

Oh, how I miss my beautiful mother.

I set the letter down and cover my face with my hands.

"Why?" I whisper, not to my mother, but to Jesus. "Why this path?"

There is not an audible answer, but I hear my mother's words in my heart.

You are not alone.

His car is in his usual spot at the apartment complex, so I pull in and wearily climb out of my car, feeling emotionally exhausted.

I climb the steps, rap on the door and wait on the tiny porch.

The door opens a minute later.

"Eliza?"

Cooper is obviously surprised to see me, but he breaks out into a big smile right before meeting my eyes and then a look crosses his face and he just reaches out a hand to me.

I go right in for the hug.

Cooper gives the best hugs. Always has.

"Let's go for a walk," Cooper says, after a minute. "Let me grab my keys." He goes inside and is back out in a couple of seconds.

We walk down the stairs and he nods to the right. "There's a little bike trail through here next to the creek," he says. "Shouldn't be too buggy yet."

We start walking and I take a deep breath, shoving my hands into the pockets of my jeans. I can feel Cooper looking over at me a few times, but I'm trying to put my thoughts into words, so I don't say anything yet.

I think he picks up on my need for some silent company. So we walk. We turn right on the path that leads along the creek. The trees are thick with leaves and the creek is steadily flowing after the snow we got this winter. Occasionally, a biker flies past us, but otherwise, it's super quiet except for the creek.

It's so peaceful right here.

My brain is going a million miles a minute and I wish I could get it to slow down so I could dissect each thought. I watch the creek and try to take some deep breaths.

Jesus, help me think.

"Eliza?"

I look over at Cooper and his brown eyes are dark with worry. "What can I do?" he asks me. "How can I help?"

"Help me process," I say.

"Definitely."

"I opened the letter from Mom this morning. I took it to the cemetery." I don't even know if Cooper knows what I'm talking about. I don't think I ever told him about the letter.

"Oh Eliza."

And in Cooper-fashion, he apparently knows.

"You went there by yourself?" he asks me.

I nod and I can feel the tears building again.

"You should have called me."

"I needed to do it."

"I know."

"I wish they could come back."

"I know."

"I need to talk to Mom."

Cooper nods. "What did the letter say?"

"Lots of things." Her words are etched deeply into my heart, into my mind. I want to tell him but I feel like if I say the words out loud, it will somehow mar the hallowedness of it.

Cooper must get it because he doesn't press me to talk about it. So we keep walking, keep listening to the creek.

I hear my mom's words.

Do not make the mistake of tossing aside the diamond, be it rough, in your hand for the rhinestone on the shelf.

What did that even mean?

"She wrote me one too, you know," Cooper says quietly, so quietly that I almost miss his words in the babbling of the creek.

"She what?"

"A letter. I got one too."

I gape at him. "You never told me."

"You never asked."

"When?"

"She gave it to me right before she died. That and a box of all my junk I'd left at your house over the years." He smiles and rubs the back of his neck. "Never realized how much stuff I had laying around there."

"What did it say?" I ask.

He looks over at me and the look in his eyes makes something in my stomach drop. He bites his lip like he's going to say something and then slightly shakes his head and keeps walking, pushing his hands into his pockets as well.

I stop on the path, fighting the tears. "Cooper?"

He turns and looks at me. "Yeah?"

"I'm sorry I pushed you away."

I'm not sure how he does it, but one minute he's standing there in front of me, looking at me with such a gentle expression and the next, he's pulled me in tight against his chest, tucking my head into the spot just under his chin.

"It's okay, Lyzie," he says into my hair.

"It's not though." I shake my head and pull back, but he reaches for my hands. "I just couldn't lose you too."

"Eliza, you will never lose me."

"You can't say that. You don't know that."

Cooper reaches for my face. "Eliza, look at me."

I close my eyes tight and I can feel the tears on my cheeks. I finally can look at him and he's looking at me with an expression I've never seen before on his face.

"I don't know what God has for the future," Cooper says. "And who am I to say whether it includes you or I living for a long time or living for just a short while longer. I just know that I have loved you for as long as I can remember. And if God allows it, I want to grow old with you. I want to marry you and have babies with you and be up to our elbows in kid messes with you."

I'm full on crying now.

"Eliza?"

I don't know what to say. I don't know when it happened or how it happened or if it's always been there and I just never noticed it, but somehow, someway, as quietly as it could come, my old friend has become so much more.

I think about Ashten and she called it so long ago. And I think about my mom and how she knew, even then.

"Mom's letter?" I ask Cooper.

He nods. "She told me to never give up."

"And to never surrender?"

He grins and his thumbs rub over my cheekbones. "I love you, Eliza."

"I love you too, Cooper."

And as he leans down to kiss me, I know.

Maybe all adventures aren't in exciting places or across oceans or mountains. Maybe the "great, wide somewhere" doesn't always hold the answers. Maybe, just maybe, there can be the biggest, sweetest adventure found here, right beside my best friend.

No matter what happens, I will be content here.

THE *End*

Don't miss the continuing story in Happily Ever Ashten, *coming Winter 2016!*

CPSIA information can be obtained
at www.ICGtesting.com
Printed in the USA
LVOW01s0847021016
507014LV00022B/1409/P